Once, in Golders Green ...

# Once, in Golders Green ...

ROHAN KRIWACZEK

Duckworth Overlook

First published in the UK in 2013 by
Duckworth Overlook
90-93 Cowcross Street, London EC1M 6BF
Tel: 020 7490 7300
Fax: 020 7490 0080
info@duckworth-publishers.co.uk
www.ducknet.co.uk

The right of Rohan Kriwaczek to be identified as the Author of
the Work has been asserted by him in accordance with
the Copyright, Designs and Patents Act 1988.

A catalogue record for this book is available
from the British Library

ISBN 978 0 7156 4499 7

Printed and bound in Great Britain by
CPI Group (UK) Ltd, Croydon, Surrey

# Contents

Once, in Golders Green ...     9

The Suitcase by the Door     31

All Hail Zigg     41

A Fool Will Stay a Fool     51

The Miraculous Rabbi Feldman     59

Klezmer     89

Oskar Brantwein Gets a Present     101

One Day in Jerusalem ...     107

Postscript     141

*For Paul and Jeannette Kriwaczek*

# Once, in Golders Green ...

It was like an old joke.

'Doctor, Doctor, I keep dreaming I'm Jewish.'

Dr Mitchell, a bald, ruddy-faced man in his sixties, barely contained by his pinstriped waistcoat, flicked through my file; then suddenly his head popped up, and he fixed me with a look of triumph.

'That's nothing,' he retorted, 'last night I dreamt I was Presbyterian!" And he erupted in a torrent of self-congratulatory laughter.

Of course I should have expected exactly that. Dr Mitchell was one of those men who see every statement as an opportunity for a punchline, which was entertaining enough down the Cat and Mustard Pot on a Thursday evening, but a little disquieting in his surgery. I left the consultation with a recommendation for herbal sleeping pills and a feeling that I hadn't been taken entirely seriously.

Three months later Dr Mitchell died, not of the heart attack that everyone expected, but of a hydromorphone overdose which raised many more questions than it answered.

He was replaced by Dr Andrews, a waspish, sharp-nosed, middle-aged woman with short reddish hair and the manner of a TV prison governess. Realising that this particular problem was more psychological than physical, I thought, admittedly dubiously, that I might have more luck with a female doctor, and so, around six months after the first consultation, six months during which the dreams had, if anything, become more vivid and disturbing, and had led to serious insomnia, I made a second appointment.

This time my opening statement was taken a little more seriously. She reached for a notepad and pen, scribbled something down, then looked back at me.

'Sephardi or Ashkenazy?'

That threw me somewhat.

'Err, Ashkenazy I suppose.'

She wrote in her notebook.

'Orthodox, Liberal or Reform?'

'I'm really not sure.'

'Well do you have those side-lock things? In the dreams, I mean.'

'No ...'

'Do you go you to synagogue, eat kosher, believe in God?'

'I think so, sometimes, maybe ... they're all different.'

'So how do you know you are Jewish?'

I was rather taken aback by that. I'd never really thought about it. I just knew.

'It's a thing,' I said after some thought, 'a feeling ... sometimes it's obvious, other times more of an undercurrent, but I know it's there, it's the point ... the point of the dream ...'

'Hmm ...' More notes were made.

'And you find this disturbing?'

'Well, yes ...'

'Can I ask why?'

'I don't really know. But it's ... um ... I've never thought of myself as Jewish ... But now it's got so I can't sleep. I lie there and my heart starts pounding in anticipation'.

'Hmm.' She looked back at my file.

'It says here that you are circumcised ...'

'Yes, well my parents were sort-of Jewish I guess.'

'So then you *are* Jewish.'

'I suppose so ... ethnically.'

'Ethnically?' ·

'Well, we were never religious ... Never went to a synagogue, or did any Jewish stuff. Really Christmas was the big thing when I was a child.'

'I see ...' She turned back to her pad and spent an uncomfortably long time making notes.

'And when did the dreams start?'

'About a year ago now. Soon after I moved here.'

She looked at my file again.

'And you used to live in ... London?'

'Yes, Golders Green.'

'That's a bit of a Jewish area isn't it?'

'Not really. Well, yes, there are a fair few. But lots of normal people too. Like me.'

'Hmm ... normal ...' She muttered this under her breath whilst making a few more notes. 'And what was it brought you here, to Dorset?'

'I always planned to move out to the country, since I was a boy. And then a few years ago one of my books was made into a film. I am a writer you know.' I said this with a retrospectively embarrassing degree of pride.

'Oh?' Suddenly she seemed interested. 'Anything I might have heard of?'

'It's called *Zombie Sex-Slaves Bite Back* ... The book was called *I Can't Kill It!* They changed the title, for the film, you know, to sex it up a little.'

She looked disappointed.

'It did well in Eastern Europe ... Nearly paid for the house ...'

She continued to look disappointed, perhaps a little moreso.

'I am a horror writer,' I added, as if an explanation were necessary.

'I see.' She made a few more notes.

'So ... and what is it that you hope to get from me?'

'I was thinking you might give me something to help me sleep.'

'Hmm.' There was a very long silence.

'I'm not convinced that sleeping is the real issue here.' She pinned me with a sudden look that took me back to when I was eight, sitting in the headmistress's office, awaiting sentence after some minor transgression or other, and I shivered slightly, then tried to disguise it with a shrug, but it was too late, she had spotted it, and made another note.

'I'm going to refer you to a colleague of mine, Dr Herman. He specialises in neuroses and anxiety issues. But I know he has a long waiting list. Of course, since you've *come into money*', this was said with the tone of an accusation, 'you might want to consider seeing him privately.'

———

Okay, so I am painting this as something of a joke, but it was becoming really quite serious. By then my sleep was so disrupted on so regular a basis that I was starting to lose perspective. Normally I would get to sleep okay, but would wake up an hour or so later in a cold sweat, the last ripples of dream-world still swishing around my head. It wasn't that the dreams were particularly disturbing, not in themselves; nor were they particularly Jewish, really. But they were particularly vivid, and, as I had tried to explain to Dr Andrews, the Jewish bit, though usually an undercurrent, somehow felt like the point. What was most striking was that I was always someone else. For example, in one recurring dream I was an old Jewish man, unpacking and repacking a suitcase full of junk; in another a young violinist playing Jewish tunes in the street; I was a Jewish watchmaker dismantling a pocket watch (yes, I know, something of a cliché – but it was a dream); a disenchanted Jew staring eye to eye at a great eagle, believing it to be an angel; or a young Jewish boy playing Jews and Nazis with his mates in the back-alleys of Golders Green. And often there was a secret involved; something was hidden, or lost, or found. In each case I really felt I *was* the person, with their thoughts and their feelings, their physicality even (I am not blessed with what you would describe as a sporting physique). And often, when I woke, suddenly in the middle of the night, they left me momentarily confused as to who *I* was. That's what I found so disturbing. Strangely though, I never dreamt I was a woman, or a girl, which is a shame, as that would have been interesting. I do not understand the ladies at all, as my ex-wife would testify. After a while I found I couldn't get to sleep in the first place for fear of the dreams. And when eventually, hours later, I finally drifted off without realising it, they would rise up, even more vivid than usual, as if to punish me for trying to evade them.

In those long wakeful hours my rationality deserted me; I would find myself believing the craziest of things, offering myself the strangest of explanations for this Jewish sleeplessness, often involving ghosts or spirits, reincarnation, curses, God, even aliens, and each of them believed implicitly at the time, and sometimes on well into the daylight.

Now you might think that being a horror writer I am a man prone to fits of imagination, and no doubt that is the case with some, there are enough of us, but I can assure you that is not the case with me. My contribution to the genre is one of cool-blooded commercial calculation. Horror is, after all, largely a formulaic genre, and I have a good eye for spotting gaps in the market. I was the first to cross mutant-insect-exploitation with zombie-erotica to create zombie-insectoid-erotica, a genre now with four exponents world-wide, including myself. But certainly I have never found myself believing in such nonsense, or any nonsense really. I am cruelly rational by nature, or so my ex-wife's lawyer stated in the divorce petition. Given all that then, you might understand why these dreams, and the subsequent insanity they produced, were causing me considerable concern, and hence why I found myself in the doctor's surgery, not being taken entirely seriously, and to be fair, not really presenting myself so seriously, most likely out of embarrassment.

One thing I was sure of: I was not going to spend good money on seeing a head-doctor. I had enough experience of such people when I was a child: my father was a psychiatrist and I had been sent to various colleagues of his whenever my rebellions hit the mark. Certainly I would not be going there again under any circumstances. I suspect that is why I became a writer of schlock-horror; it represents the very opposite of his hopes for me, and, truth be told, in most of my books the biggest monster is really him, thinly disguised as a crazed scientist, or mutant-insectoid-arse-rapist – if they were alive today he and his colleagues would certainly have something to say about that.

But, nonetheless, some of Dr Andrews' more pointed questions had given me cause for thought, mostly because I couldn't answer them – the Jewish ones that is. I knew virtually nothing about Jews, beyond what I had seen in films. And, as any horror fan will testify, the scariest monsters are those that are intangible, mysterious, unknown. As soon as you see the monster face-on it loses its power. So I thought that maybe the next step should be to learn a bit more about them, what they do, what they think, what they are; a task that would have been easy when I was still living in Golders Green and quite uninterested, but here, in Chetnole, a one-shop village in the heart of white-middle-class-elderly-English Dorset, and still under a driving ban, it was to prove a little more of a challenge.

Naturally my first stop was the internet, but all it revealed was that I didn't know what I was searching for. I mean, what do I type in? Jews? Jewish? I tried questions: what is being Jewish about? What does Jewish mean? What are Jews? And found myself swamped with one-million-seven-hundred-and-eighteen-thousand-four-hundred-and-thirty-nine opinions delivered in zero-point-three-one seconds. It was clear what I really needed was to talk to someone in the know. One thing I did learn was that the nearest synagogue was in Bournemouth, and I was damned if I was going that far out of my way. Finally, in desperation, I turned to the local phone book. That was how I came to call Rabbi Kraven.

Our first conversation went something like this:

*'Hello.'* His voice was thin, wispy, the voice of an elderly man. It later turned out that I had just caught him on a bad day, and he was only around sixty. But for the purposes of this conversation I imagined him to be around eighty.

'Hello, is that Rabbi Kraven?'

*'Who is this calling?'* There was the hint of an accent, possibly more of an intonation, but I couldn't place it anywhere specific.

'Er, you don't know me, my name's Rohan Kriwaczek.'

*'What?'*

'Rohan Kriwaczek. My name.'

*'Yes. What do you want?'*

'Am I talking to Rabbi Kraven?' I should explain that my local telephone directory is around fifteen years old so I can never be sure I am talking to the right person.

*'I would assume so. Are you?'*

'Yes ... I think so.'

*'Then get on with it. What do you want?'*

'Err, I'm not really sure.'

There was a pause.

Finally he said, *'I'm sorry, this isn't the call I was expecting,'* and hung up, leaving me more puzzled than before.

I might have left it at that, but he was the only person listed under the title rabbi within a twenty-mile radius, and happened to live in Thornford, a village just a half hour's bike ride up the road. But it was clear I needed to plan what I was going to say a little better, and so decided to sleep on it. Of course, as might have been predicted, I had an intolerable night of wakefulness punctuated by occasional momentary dreams and sudden cold sweats: I was an old man with a wooden leg, telling made-up tales about how I survived the holocaust; then a trendy young DJ, trying to get the punters excited by my Jewish wedding tunes drum'n'bass mix. And I can assure you it's not as funny as it sounds. So it was with some trepidation that I called him again the following evening.

*'Hello?'* This time his voice was a little stronger, though still clearly suspicious.

'Hello, is that Rabbi Kraven?'

*'Who is this calling?'*

'Please don't hang up, rabbi. This is Rohan Kriwaczek. I called you last night.'

*'Last night? You are the idiot?'*

'I'm sorry?'

*'The idiot who called last night. Who didn't know what he wanted.'*

'Err yes, yes, that was me.'

*'So, what do you want tonight?'*

'I want to talk to you.'

*'You are talking to me. But am I sure I want to talk to you?'*

'No, I mean face to face. I was hoping I could come and see you.'

*'To talk about what? You don't seem to be saying anything very interesting.'*

'About being Jewish.'

*'And are you Jewish?'*

'Err, no, well, yes, I think so, I don't really know ...'

*'Then let me help you. If you were Jewish you wouldn't be calling me on the Sabbath, but then if I were Jewish, and I am, I wouldn't be answering the phone, and I did. So maybe we are both Jewish, and maybe we both aren't. Who knows? In the end haShem will judge us all, and then maybe it will be sorted out. Until then ...'*

'Please Rabbi Kraven, this is serious, I haven't slept properly for over a year now and I need your help.' I know I sounded desperate, but really I was.

*'And what does this have to do with me?'*

'Nothing, to do with you. But it's definitely something to do with being Jewish.'

*'I don't understand. You don't know if you're Jewish, but you can't sleep because you're Jewish ...'*

'No, it's the dreams. I keep dreaming that I'm Jewish, and not me, I'm other Jewish people, all kinds of people, but all Jewish ... And I think maybe it's a sign of some kind, that I need to find out more.'

*'And I think maybe you are a little bit crazy. But then, maybe you are also saying something a little bit interesting. Crazy people do sometimes say interesting things, after all.'*

'So I can come and see you then?'

*'I am sure you can.'*

'Perhaps tomorrow, after lunch?'

*'I'm always here.'*

'Shall we say about three o'clock?'

'I'll leave that to you.'

'Well, okay, three o'clock. Thank you. I'll see you then.'

The rabbi hung up.

———

That night, during only two hours of what could loosely be described as sleep, I had a particularly vivid and disturbing dream. I was a rabbi, mumbling prayers to myself whilst a thug held a gun to my head; as he pulled the trigger I shat myself, and woke in a panic, checking my bedding. After that I gave up and sat on the internet trying to find references to Rabbi Kraven, but there were none. (I always like to look people up before meeting them.) By the time I set out for my appointment I was, needless to say, utterly exhausted.

———

Rabbi Kraven lived about half a mile beyond Thornford, up a long tree-lined gravel track, so deeply grooved and rutted that I soon decided to chain up my bike and make the remaining two hundred yards on foot. I had often cycled this track but never really noticed it before. Generally around here it is unpolitic to go exploring paths that aren't clearly labelled *public*. With some effort, for my limbs were as tired as my brain despite the apparent rest they might have had, I followed the track up the hill, frost crunching under my feet, and increasingly unsure if this could be the right place. Then suddenly there it was on my left, a run-down little cottage, half hidden behind a row of cypresses, with a thin stream of grey wafting from its chimney, promising warmth.

Surprised at how nervous I was, I took a deep breath and knocked. After what felt like minutes there was a muffled shuffling on the other side, followed by the click of locks being turned and the door creaked open. The sight that greeted me did not disappoint. Rabbi Kraven looked every bit the part: the long grey beard and twisted side-locks, the small round skullcap, the ill-fitting black suit in a strangely old-fashioned cut, the white tassels hanging out under his jacket; it was all there, even the slightly oversized nose. Not to mention the somewhat disdainful expression on his face. All just as I remembered from the Orthodox Jews that lived two doors down when I was a child. Though this was the first time I had ever spoken to one, at least face to face.

'Hello,' I stuttered, not really knowing what to say.

'Yes? What do you want?!' he replied, more as an accusation than a question.

'Err, I'm Rohan Kriwaczek. I spoke to you yesterday ...'

'Ah yes, the idiot. I suppose you should come in then.'

He stepped out of the way and beckoned me inside, momentarily breaking the severity of his expression with the slightest hint of a smile.

The door opened onto a long, low-ceilinged room, crowded with dark mahogany furniture and an overwhelming smell of damp and smoke. At one end was a dining room table piled high with books, newspapers and a stack of dirty plates and cutlery; at the other a fireplace, and two worn-out leather armchairs. Every inch of wall space was taken up with either bookshelves or paintings on Jewish themes – a dancing fiddler, Jerusalem at dusk, and many pictures of elderly rabbis reading at their desks. Despite the bright daylight outside, the room was surprisingly dark, lit by a couple of dim table lamps at either end and the glow from the fire. The rabbi sat in one of the armchairs and gestured that I should take the other. I started taking my coat off, but found it was still pretty cold inside, despite the fire, and hesitated.

'Yes, it's the damp,' he said, having noticed my pause. 'Makes it impossible to warm the place. Best keep your coat on. I'd offer you a cup of tea, but my kettle is broken. Perhaps you would like some schnapps?'

Now I am never one to turn down the offer of a drink, as my ex-wife also testified, and particularly in a situation like this where ice is in urgent need of being broken, so I accepted the offer with restrained enthusiasm. The rabbi reached across to a cupboard on his left and brought out a bottle of Talisker whisky, one of my favourites, and two cut-glass tumblers.

'Mine is a humble house,' he said as he poured the drinks, 'but I always keep a bottle in case of visitors ... And you, you are the first for some time.'

I commended him on his choice of distilleries and we both took a drink. I downed mine in one gulp and he immediately refilled it.

'So, Mr Rohan Kriwaczek, I hope you have by now worked out what it is you want to ask me about.'

I had, but my brain was so muddled with exhaustion that it came out in a garbled incoherent stream that even I couldn't follow. Honestly, he must have thought I was crazy. Insomnia does that, makes you seem crazy: it was as if the sense inside my head hadn't the energy to survive the outside world; whenever I tried to express it the words sounded plain ridiculous, and wrong. After a few minutes looking rather bemused he slowed me down and asked me to start again, from the beginning, in clear chronological steps. So I began again with the dreams, how vivid they were, how they all have the Jewish thing in common, and how they were stopping me from sleeping; and that I wanted to know my enemy, perhaps not the best choice of words but I think he understood what I meant, as he nodded periodically throughout.

'So you want me to tell you what being Jewish is about?' he summarised once I had finished.

'Yes,' I replied hesitantly, and he burst into uproarious laughter.

'That, young man, is an impossible question. I could tell you what being Jewish is about for me. I have some idea what it meant for the great rabbis of old ...' and he gestured to the paintings all around, 'but for you? That I cannot say.'

He refilled my glass.

'But I can tell you one thing ...' Again he waved his hand at the room. 'All these books, they are each asking the same question, in their own way. So perhaps then I can answer you. Perhaps being Jewish is about asking what being Jewish is about.' And he smiled. 'You see? It was easy after all.'

'But rabbi ... should I call you rabbi?'

'You can call me Moses if you like ... I know, a rather grand name for a broken, crooked old man like me.'

'Okay, well, Moses, what about the dreams?'

He seemed to think for a while. Then looked back at me directly.

'Tell me Mr Rohan Kriwaczek, what do you think a rabbi is?'

'Umm ...' I was rather taken aback by this unexpected question. 'I assume you're like a priest, but for Jews.'

At that the rabbi smiled.

'Not at all. We are very different creatures. A priest is part of a great organisation imposed upon a community. A Catholic priest is in direct line with God, or so they claim. But either way, priests are a mouthpiece for a greater whole, and always allied to a specific theology. That's how they get their churches. Their congregations. They are like MPs really. Some are backbenchers, some set their sights on the cabinet, but they all have a party, a theology. And they all preach the agreed word of God.

'Now rabbis, we do not preach, we discuss. We are nobody's mouth-piece. To be a rabbi is simply to be wise, specifically in Jewish law, but also wise about people, wise about the world, the way things are. As for God, it is not for us to understand the ways of haShem. Not even the greatest of rabbis would claim that. All we can do is ponder, consider, and discuss.'

'Yes, but the dreams …?'

'Please, be patient. It has been a long time since I last had a student in my house. Allow me my little indulgences. Let me do this the Jewish way.

'Where was I? Oh yes, we ponder, we consider, but always with our feet set firmly on the ground. Sure, it's about knowing the difficult stuff, the books, the law, but really it's a conversation, between all the learned stuff and the world around. And often it all comes down to seeing-the-bleedin'-obvious.

'Now you have come here to see me, no doubt mistaking me for some kind of Jewish priest and wanting me to exorcise you of your Jewish-related insomnia. That is how you see it. Am I right?'

'I suppose so, sort of.' That wasn't actually quite how I saw it but was a close enough fit.

'Now this isn't rabbi stuff, this is more cod-psychology, but that's okay. People rarely want rabbi stuff these days. So this is how I see it, seeing the obvious, as it were.

'You are a self-hating Jew, from a family of self-hating Jews. Oh, there are a great many of you around. I understand, believe me, there is a lot to be disenchanted about. Anyway, for years you lived in Golders Green, from childhood, surrounded by proud Jews, many of them wearing their various traditions quite literally on their sleeves, or their heads perhaps, and so every day you were reminded of what you felt you weren't, and that became part of your identity. It became so deeply embedded that you stopped noticing it years ago. Like a reflex. But then you moved to the Dorset countryside, a land devoid of Jews, and now this reflex inside you has nothing to kick out against, so every night it sets about invent-ing Jews as you sleep. Of course, they are all pieces of you, finding their way up to the surface. Yes? Does that sound about right? And this reflex leads you to seek me out too. Am I close?'

'Err, well, I'd have to think about it ... maybe ... I don't know ...'

'Well, even so, you came here hoping for a cure, for the dreams, yes?' He didn't wait for my answer. 'Well I think I have an idea. What you need is some empathy.'

'Empathy?'

'Yes. Empathy. These dreams that you fear so much, the way you describe them they are like fragments of stories, and you, you claim to be a writer. So really, it is the obvious, as I said: you should write the stories: know your enemy, like you say. And what better way to know your enemy than to write their story. And in doing that you find empathy, for them, for yourself, and the fear will be gone. And then you will sleep. It is the bleedin' obvious.'

'But I'm not that kind of writer. I write horror, schlock-horror.'

'Surely it's all the same thing really. The same skills and techniques apply.'

I tried to restrain my irritation at the ignorance of this comment, and patiently explained, in simple terms, why what he was suggesting was ridiculous, that really they were quite different things altogether, and that I wouldn't know where to begin.

'So,' he said, 'turn them into, what did you say, schlock-horror. The world could do with a few more good Jewish ghost stories.'

Again I restrained my irritation and explained the difference between horror and ghost genres. He looked a little disappointed at my reaction and for some reason I felt the need to placate him.

'The truth is,' I said with the tone of someone reluctantly admitting his own failings, 'I'm not a very skilled writer. I'm good at what I do, but I know my limits. And they pretty much start and finish at schlock-horror. Really I know nothing about Jews or being Jewish, and very little about empathy either, as my ex-wife would attest.'

He sighed.

'Yes, the breakup of a marriage is a tragic thing. But you know, Mr Rohan Kriwaczek, you are wrong about much of this. You are wrong about your limitations, as people always are; you are wrong about empathy, that you are here at all demonstrates that; and you are wrong about being Jewish, for really you know as much about that as any of us. It seems to me, for whatever reason, that you are being invited to join the conversation. Maybe it's God, or your own unconscious, or karma, call it what you will, that isn't important. What is important is that you look into your heart and say your piece. For that, I think, is what being Jewish is really about: a great conversation among Jews of all types, even self-haters like you, about what being Jewish is about. Do you see? That's what all these books are. That is what I've spent my life studying.'

Again he waved at the many shelves, and again I protested, this time saying something stupid about asking Ramone to play the Paganini guitar concerto, as if the rabbi would know the Ramones, and come to think of it, I'm not sure Paganini wrote a guitar concerto, but he seemed very pleased with his idea and wasn't going to let it go.

'Honestly, I wouldn't know where to start,' I repeated for the fourth or fifth time.

'Start with something simple, *once upon a time* or *once, in Golders Green ...* and take it from there. Come on, I'm being a little facetious but you know what I'm saying, you're not a fool; an idiot, maybe, but not a fool.'

'Now,' he said, pushing himself up out of the low armchair with some effort, 'I really must return to my evening's studies.'

'Of course,' and I too stood and followed him to the door.

'You know,' he said as we crossed the crowded room, 'what I was saying, it's just a thought, take it or leave it. But I do think it might help you to write them down, the dreams I mean. If only for yourself.' He said these words with a surprising tenderness that rather took me aback and all I could do in return was smile. We shook hands and then I remembered the book I had brought, and gave it to him.

'Hmm, *I Can't Kill It* by Rohan Kriwaczek.' He looked down, studying the cover, a semi-naked zombie sex slave rending her chains, then back at me. 'Looks interesting, thank you ... And maybe one day, Rohan Kriwaczek, you will write me a good Jewish ghost story. I would like that.'

'Maybe, we'll see,' I replied, thinking the opposite.

Then, just as I was leaving he gently grabbed my arm to turn me around again and looked me severely in the eye.

'You know, young man, you remind me of the story of the slave.'

He said this with such unexpected earnestness that I can remember his expression to this day: the deep pitying eyes, the solemn mouth, as if the weight of ages had suddenly landed upon his shoulders; and then it was gone and he smiled again.

'No, of course you don't know it. Never mind. Goodbye Rohan Kriwaczek.'

I'm not sure how I felt as I cycled back across the by then dark and frozen Dorset countryside. Certainly I had liked the rabbi, found him positively entertaining even, though I was also a little affronted at his blind assertions about how I should lead my life and career. But then I suppose I should have expected nothing less from a rabbi. And I was also somewhat perplexed by that last comment of his, about the story of the slave, not so much in itself but for the way he said it. But yes, overall he was the first proper full-on Jew I had ever spoken to, and I thought it had gone pretty well. He no longer seemed like an enemy. I guess in some ways I felt I had faced my demons and found them to be a rather charming and unassuming eccentric old man. Or rather, that's what I hoped. And in any case, he would make an excellent model for a Van Helsing-style monster hunter. I was, however, pretty sure I wouldn't be visiting him again.

It wasn't until I got home that I realised how cold I was. I turned the heating on to full, made myself a large hot toddy, followed by an even larger bacon and cheese sandwich, and settled down to watch Saturday evening television. By nine o'clock my eyes were starting to droop, which wasn't unusual given my general state of near-delusional exhaustion, but on this occasion, what with the events of the day, and my complete disinterest in whatever it was I was watching, I decided to take the risk and head to bed.

That night my hopes were richly rewarded with a long and dreamless sleep that lasted right through to two o'clock the following afternoon.

———

One of the remark-worthy things about insomnia is how quickly it can be dispelled by a good night's sleep. I know that may sound obvious, but honestly, after months on end of troubled nights eating away at your sanity, leading you down paths of creeping paranoia and often frankly ludicrous delusions, to wake up refreshed, with a clear and steady mind is not unlike being reborn, or at least coming home after a long and traumatic holiday. Suddenly the dread and desperation was simply gone, and the world once again made its usual sense. Within days the whole sorry saga was virtually forgotten, and when I did think about it I was largely baffled. I mean, what was I making such a fuss about? Most of all I couldn't believe I had gone so far as to visit a rabbi. Thinking back now, it seems obvious that my sudden sleepfulness must have had something to do with Rabbi Kraven, maybe something he said, or just talking to a full-on Jew face to face, who knows, but at the time I didn't give it a second thought; just another sign of how unaccountably crazy I had become. Within a few restful nights the insomnia and everything it entailed was almost entirely forgotten, and certainly no longer of any concern.

Of more concern was an upcoming deadline. For nearly a year I had been without the will to write and now had only three months left to deliver *I Can't Kill Them*, the third in the *I Can't Kill It* trilogy. But at last, with my energy renewed, I felt able to get down to it and was soon writing again, and at quite a pace, for me at least, a thousand words a day, and not without some flair if I say so myself. And I cannot emphasise enough how reassuring it was to once again have my head filled with familiar thoughts of zombie-insectoid-temptresses, not to mention the fun of being Harry Hand, zombie-killer extraordinaire, something I always relish. He and I have a lot in common. We're both Sagittarians, both have messy divorces in our past, and I like to think that were the zombie apocalypse to come I would rise to the occasion with much the same gusto. So really, as Harry Hand ventured down into the bowels of the zombie-insectoid hive to destroy the nursery of zombie-insectoid soldier eggs before they hatch, assisted only by Lisa, the lone survivor of the attack on the Roundhammer, and of course a virgin, the very last thing on my mind was Rabbi Kraven. That is until the dreams returned.

This time they were different, less vivid, and less disturbing really, though whether that was a change in the dreams themselves or a change in me is hard to know. Either way, they didn't seem to stop me from sleeping as they had before, so that was a big improvement. It was the same cast of characters but the storylines, if dreams can be said to have storylines, were all muddled with Harry Hand's zombie adventures, which made them altogether more entertaining. I was an old Jewish man, unpacking and packing a suitcase, just as before, but this time, I was aware that *they* were coming. Suddenly in burst a troop of zombie-insectoid soldier-mites, who dragged me off to their hive. I was very aware of not losing hold of the suitcase and somehow managed to keep it with me, all the way to the mutant-digestion-pool. Then, just as the queen was about to infect me with her hypodermic nipple-mandible, I woke, not in a cold sweat, but with a broad grin and nearly laughed out loud. I had never dreamt my books before and found it really rather thrilling. It was the same with the other dreams. They would start as before, in suburban Golders Green, and end in the hive. Sometimes Lisa would come to my rescue, and on one occasion we even kissed, though sadly I woke before things could progress any further. In any case, the recurrence of the dreams did turn my thoughts back to Rabbi Kraven and what he had said on that wintry afternoon, particularly the comment he made as I left, about the story of the slave.

And then the book was done, finished, sent off to my editor, and I was once again between projects, with too much time on my hands and too much space in my head.

'Time for a well-deserved holiday,' my agent said, meaning 'I haven't yet managed to sell any of your other proposals'.

So it was just as an absent-minded exercise that I set about writing Rabbi Kraven his ghost story, to keep the wheels turning, so to speak. And perhaps I really just wanted an excuse to go and visit him again. Not because of the dreams, which no longer bothered me much, though they were still there, but because I wanted to ask him about that comment, *the story of the slave*. He had said it with such sudden earnestness; a mixture of pity, compassion, and perhaps a little condemnation. It had started to haunt me if only a little: that look in his eyes; the way he had tugged at my sleeve. I tried looking up slaves on www.oldtestamentonlline.re but couldn't find any relevant stories, to my mind anyway. But all the same I didn't want to go back there empty-handed. Not that I owed him anything, but even so.

It wasn't one of my best. As I had tried to explain to the rabbi, ghost stories are all about psychological horror, and I am a just not a psychological writer; my monsters are have always been physical and the threat they pose a physical threat. That I can do. But so far as I can see the only real danger a ghost could pose is that you might injure yourself tripping over whilst running away. But still I tried. It was the tale of a Viennese synagogue haunted by an SS officer killed in the building during the war, whose ghost was doomed to attend services and religious study classes for all eternity, or for at least as long as the synagogue remained standing, I don't think it was quite clear on that. Anyway, in the end an elderly rabbi, much like Rabbi Kraven, having been convinced of the ghost's sincere remorse for his appalling crimes whilst alive, sets him free by offering him a Jewish blessing, but, as his spirit leaves, the synagogue begins to shake and then crumbles into dust, for it had itself been bombed during the war, and it was only God's will to punish the officer that had kept it standing.

As I say, not a great tale, but I was quite pleased with bits of it, particularly my characterisation of the rabbi, who, when talking, never seemed to get to the point, and when he did it was always a different point to the one expected. The story never made it to publication. Apparently ghost stories are considered rather old-fashioned. I did get one offer, if I could rewrite it as a Jewish vampire story, but the publisher, a small American press, was closed down a few months later pending undisclosed federal charges.

And so it was one bright spring afternoon that I found myself once again parking my bicycle at the bottom of the rutted track that led up the hill to the rabbi's house. It was about five months since my first visit, and the path couldn't have looked more different. Where there had been nothing but bare branches, icicles and snow was now all richly adorned with luscious leaves of every possible green, highlighted with touches of pink, yellow and white. The ground was knee high in ferns, foxgloves, hemlock and thistles, and up above the trees all drooped with blossom. No vehicle had been here since my last visit, that was for sure, and in places there was barely space for a man to pass between the overgrown bushes. Clearly Rabbi Kraven had no interest in gardening. It was only as I reached the top of the hill that I recognised the row of cypresses, unchanged save for their previous sprinkling of snow, and perhaps a little spring growth.

I wasn't actually sure that the rabbi would be in as I hadn't managed to get through to him by phone. For some reason I kept getting the dead tone, though that isn't too uncommon in rural Dorset, particularly after a storm, and we'd had a fair few of those over the previous weeks. But he had left me with an open invitation, so there I was, on the off-chance, so to speak. As I rounded the hill I was a little disappointed not to see smoke rising up over the top of the cypresses, for though bright, it was a surprisingly chilly afternoon, and I had hoped to soon be sitting beside a warm hearth. But nonetheless, I was still optimistic that the rabbi would be in; most likely just being frugal with his wood. And so as I followed the path behind the row of trees, clutching my manuscript and a bottle of Talisker single malt, I was completely thrown by the sight that greeted me.

At first I did a double take, looking around almost desperately, thinking I must have come to the wrong place. Then, as I began to realise what I was seeing, shock and confusion pulsed through my body and my heart went into overdrive, as if trying to pound its way out of my chest. It was a good few seconds before I got my bearings and could take it all in.

The cottage was burnt to the ground. Completely destroyed. Only the walls remained upright, and they had toppled in parts. Charred timbers poked from the earth where once had stood a little wooden porch, and when I looked in through the blackened empty holes that had been windows, all I could see was a pile of half-burnt roof timbers under an open sky. I was stunned, baffled, and had no idea what I should do. And what about the rabbi? I could only hope that he had got out okay. But where would he be?

I did a brief circuit of the ruins, then sat on a chunk of collapsed wall to think. Whatever had happened it must have been a good few months ago as the brambles and ferns were already moving in. Finally I decided to head into the village and enquire.

It was with a heavy heart that I returned down the hill to my bicycle, and pedalled my way into Thornford, part hopeful, part dreading what I would find out. But whatever I might have been expecting, I was not prepared for the answers I got.

'Fire? There's been no fire round here ...'

'No, never heard of any rabbi. There was a foreign chap lived here a while ago. Came down from London but he didn't fit in quite right and went back to the city. That must have been ten years ago now. I think he was from Korea ...'

'Oh, you might mean Old Tom's cottage, that burnt down some fifteen years ago or so ...'

It was bizarre. Nobody seemed to have heard of the rabbi, and Thornford is a small village. Everyone knows everybody else's business. But I guess if he kept himself to himself, as I imagined he probably did, and his house was on the other side of the hill ... Still, it added to my general sense of bafflement, and I really didn't know what to do next. How was I going to find the rabbi? I decided to head back to his cottage, and take another look.

This time as I made my way up the hill I was filled with trepidation, part hoping that I had simply been mistaken. Perhaps I had turned up the wrong track to find a similar-looking house in ruins. But no, there it was, nothing but a burnt-out shell. I headed up the path to the front door and ventured just inside. There was no sign of any furniture, or his library, no sign of any previous habitation at all really, not even charred remains. Doubtless it had all been burnt to a cinder, and now lay under the fallen roof. Ferns and other weeds were sprouting all around amongst the muddle of tiles and blackened beams, and then something unexpectedly bright blue caught my eye amongst the brown, green and grey of the ruins. I clambered across the rubble towards the fireplace. There, on what would have been the mantelpiece, was my book.

I picked it up. Flicked through it. It was a little swollen with rain, but there was no sign of any fire damage, not even the slightest charring or smoke stain, and yet the wood on which it sat was burnt to its core. I turned to the title page to see the handwritten dedication *To Rabbi Kraven*, and my signature. For a moment I didn't know what to think, and then a sudden thrill rippled through my body and I realised: he must have been a ghost. Looking around, it became obvious: these ruins couldn't possibly be a few months old. Nature was well on its way to taking over. It had to be years. As it hit me I panicked, feeling like the foundations of my whole reality were crumbling around me, and was then seized with a fear that sent me running down the hill to my bike and peddling like a maniac all the way home. When I got in I poured myself a large Talisker and sat on the sofa, trembling, my mind spinning way beyond my control. I must have sat there for three hours and drunk half the bottle before I was even capable of standing up and turning on the television.

And that might have been the end of it. The story of how I came to drink whisky with a Jewish ghost one winter's afternoon. And it would have been a story I could live with, even take some pride in retelling, but as it turned out things weren't to prove that simple.

Over the following few weeks I did extensive research trying to track down Rabbi Kraven, but could find no reference to him whatever. I traced the owners and tenants of the cottage back to 1768 when it was built, but nobody called Kraven had ever lived there. Nor could I find any record of a Rabbi Kraven having ever been a part of Dorset's sparse Jewish community. Strangest of all, when I returned to my rather out of date telephone directory I could no longer find the listing. I spent hours searching through that book, but there was no Rabbi Kraven. The only evidence of him having ever existed was the inscription in the book I had given him, and a scrap of paper on which I had written his name and phone number.

So what was he? To be a ghost, he would have to be the ghost of someone, someone with a connection to that cottage, or so I gathered from what I read on the subject; all the theories, however wacky, agreed on that. So if there never was a Rabbi Kraven, at least not that had a connection with the cottage, he couldn't have been a ghost. I was stumped. I even went so far as to contact a number of 'psychics' and 'paranormal specialists', always anonymously, to see if they could shed any further light on the matter, but received the expected preposterous replies: one suggested it was an incubus, whose purpose, rather than to sexually corrupt me, was to convert me to Judaism; another that it was a dispossessed nature spirit, tapping into my unconscious desires to lure me, though where or into what they weren't clear. Today my best explanation is that he was some kind of psychological projection brought on by the extreme exhaustion of my insomnia, but even that doesn't really fit with the experience, and raises more questions than it answers. Nonetheless, whatever it was, delusion, fantasy, paranormal experience, call it what you will, it did make me think all the more deeply about what the rabbi had said to me. The strangeness now surrounding that afternoon only served to amplify its importance, most of all that comment about the slave.

Eventually, having exhaustedly searched the internet for some clue, to no avail, I emailed Rabbi Goldblum of the Bournemouth Liberal synagogue to ask if he knew of a story that might be relevant. He had previously been very helpful in my attempt to trace Rabbi Kraven. A few days later I received this reply:

*Dear Mr Kriwaczek,*

*Given the context you present there is one story that comes to mind.*

*Long ago in Old Jerusalem there lived a rich and successful busi-nessman. But though his business had been truly blessed, not so his family, for his wife had died in childbirth and he had rowed with his only son who now lived hundreds of miles away across the sea. And so as the old man lay dying he had only his loyal slave to tend to him.*

*News of the old man's death took many months to reach the son, and it was many months more before he made it back to Jerusalem to claim his inheritance.*

*When he knocked upon the door of his childhood home it was the slave who answered.*

*'What is it you want?' he demanded, in a gruff and unfriendly tone.*

*'How dare you speak to me like that!' replied the son. 'Do you not recognise who you are talking to? I am the son of Efraim, your master, and this is my house.'*

*'Oh I recognise you,' answered the slave. 'But you are mistaken. This is my house. In his will your father left everything to me. He asked only that I let you claim one item, of your own choice.'*

*'I do not believe you,' demanded the son. 'Show me the will at once!'*

*And so the slave went into the house and reappeared with the will, and it was all as he had said. His father had left everything to his slave, there was no doubt.*

*Distraught and not knowing what he should do, the son went to see the rabbi and showed him the will.*

*'You see,' he said, 'you see how I have been betrayed, and by my own father. What am I to do, rabbi?'*

*The rabbi carefully read through the will, and then looked up at the son, and smiled.*

*'On the contrary, young man', said the rabbi, still smiling. 'This will shows that you have a very wise and loving father. He knew that when he died it would take months for word to reach you, and months more before you would return. Had he left his estate to you, you would most likely have come back to find the slave long gone and with him much of your father's wealth too. And so he left it all to his slave, that it might be kept safe, but with the proviso that you can claim one item of his*

*property. So you see, all you have to do is claim the slave, and then all of his possessions fall to you, his rightful owner.*

*And so the son received his full inheritance after all, and being a forgiving man, he freed the slave, and gave him enough gold to make himself a decent life.*

*I hope that is helpful,*
*Sincerely,*
*Rabbi L. Goldblum*

I wasn't really sure what to make of that, though something about it made me feel it was most likely the story the rabbi, imaginary or not, had been referring to. And if so, was he suggesting that I was like the slave, thinking I owned my life, but in reality being merely a temporary custodian, or like the son, feeling cheated, and needing a rabbi to show me the way back to my inheritance? Of course I will never know, and I don't suppose it really matters. And after all, it is good to have things to ponder on those long dark winter evenings.

Soon afterwards I suddenly noticed that the dreams had stopped, and I have never had one since, not like those, not dreams where I was Jewish in the third person, as it were. I can't be sure, but I think the last one was the night before I returned to the rabbi's cottage; I don't remember any since. In a strange way I miss them now. And so, a few months ago I started doing as the rabbi had suggested, writing them down, trying to turn them into stories. Truth to tell, I have to admit I am enjoying the process and its challenges far more than I had pre-supposed, and there is even a small part of me that likes to imagine that when they are done Rabbi Kraven, wherever and whatever he is or was or may be, will somehow place a copy in his bookcase, to 'join the conversation'.

As for the ghost story I wrote him, it was really not my best work and in retrospect I'm glad it never saw the light of day.

# The Suitcase by the Door

Aaron took two plain brass candlesticks from the cupboard and set them on the marble mantelpiece. They looked awkward and out of place in such grand surroundings, but this evening was Pulkhan haTik, the ritual of the suitcase, an evening that had always been lit by those candlesticks; they had been his mother's, and his grandmother's before her, possibly going all the way back to Rabbi Levshin, his great-great-great-grandfather.

Rabbi Levshin had been an important man. His name had always been spoken with reverence. Aaron remembered his mother telling the story – how, when on his deathbed, the rabbi's eldest son had asked: 'Father, of all your wisdom, all your learning, what would you most have us remember?' And the great rabbi raised his head, looked his son square in the eye, and with his final dying breath, whispered *Der shepet bei der tir!* Aaron no longer recalled any Yiddish, that was all so long ago, a lifetime ago, but the sound of those particular words would always be with him; they had carried through the generations, becoming something of a family motto, the enigmatic answer to all his unwanted questions: 'the suitcase-by-the-door ...' And so the rabbi's descendants had taken him at his word, for he had always proven to be wise in judgement: every year, on the great man's birthday, the family would come together to show their suitcases, discuss the choice and meaning of the contents, check that everything was in good order, tell stories of the rabbi, of survival, hope and escape, and most of all to thank the Lord that this year they had not been needed – though in truth that wasn't always the case, for the rabbi's words did prove wise, and many times his descendants had had to leave, but always with a suitcase ready by the door. *And that is why each year we celebrate Pulkhan haTik, why we always keep a suitcase packed: to remember our history, and be ready for our future ...* It's funny, Aaron thought, as he pottered about making his various preparations for

31

the evening: he could remember every detail of the story, every word, even his Mother's accent, and yet she would have been speaking to him in Yiddish, so why did he remember it in English? And he smiled to himself. Yes, the human brain truly is a remarkable organ.

Almost everything was in its place now: he had covered the coffee table with his finest embroidered tablecloth, and laid out a decanter of schnapps (in this case a 25-year-old Highland malt) and some 'celebratory' food. He didn't really eat in the evenings any more, but Milano, his *man*, had prepared some pastrami and cheese sandwiches before leaving. Aaron always gave Milano the night off on Pulkhan haTik. He preferred to spend that evening alone with his thoughts. It was a night for history and contemplation, for remembering who he had once been. No, Milano has no place here tonight. Tonight is for Mama, and he glanced across at the mantelpiece, where her photo smiled back at him reassuringly.

All that remained were the final details. He took the candlesticks with him to the sofa where he began to polish them. He didn't know why, but he always got them out first, and placed them on either side of Mama, like squat little brass sentries, to watch him prepare. It was the way he had always done it, so far as he could remember. It felt right. Finally he fitted each with a fresh candle, placed them in the centre of the table, and lit them. Only one thing remained. He heaved himself up and, and with a sudden and surprising feeling of ceremony, made his way to the entrance hall. There he pulled a medium-sized battered old leather suitcase from the back of the large Georgian wardrobe that stood beside the porch door, not without some effort, and carried it back to the living room, placing it carefully, ritualistically, on the floor beside the table, just so. Now everything was ready. He set himself down on the sofa once again, poured himself a glass of schnapps and switched off the lights, using the remote control.

'Hmm ... To Life! ... To Wealth! ... And to never having to go anywhere I don't bloody want to go!' And he took a large gulp of the fiery liquid, spluttering a little in the aftershock. The room looked very different by candlelight. Everything backed into darkness. On the far wall he could just make out the gold mouldings of picture frames glimmering faintly, but the paintings themselves were all but black. Only the table in front of him was clearly illuminated, an oasis of flickering orange light against the white of the tablecloth. It reminded him of his child-hood, of the evenings Mama would sit him at the high table, and tell him stories of Rabbi Levshin and his wise words. And then they would eat soup with special dumplings, and sing songs. He took a minute to savour the reminiscence. Then, with much gravity, opened the suitcase, and carefully placed each item in its correct space on the table, all the while thinking back to his childhood, to his earliest memories, to the first time he had become interested in Pulkhan haTik. That was the year his grandfather had come across from the old country.

It must have been nineteen thirty-seven or eight, he wasn't sure – (was he seventy-eight or nine this year?) He remembered being sat beside Mama, crouched in front of the stove, in their tiny little kitchen off Brick Lane. Zayde, his grandfather, was sitting the other side of the stove. He was barely visible in the darkness, but the regular creaking of the rocking chair spoke of his presence. Mama had already told the story of Rabbi Levshin and was now presenting the contents of her case, at that moment a little tin box filled with needles and thread, when Zayde suddenly erupted 'What are you filling the poor boy's head with all that shit for? For God's sake teach the boy something useful!' This resulted in a great row, until finally, having been beaten down, and having no other place to go, Mama descended into a sulk where she sat.

'You listen to me, son. I've done my share of getting away, living in hiding, all that shit. Let me show you what I keep in my bag. Five things. That's all you need ...' And he took them out, one by one, laying them on the floor in front of Aaron. 'A blanket ... a good knife, strong enough to split a log, sharp enough to slice an onion ... a tinder box, with some good dry tinder ... a spare pair of boots ... and a couple of packets of cigarettes – for currency! That's all you'll ever need, if you know how to use them, mind. If not, then you're fucked whatever's in your bag.

'I'll tell you what son, I'll teach you how to sharpen a knife, and once you can do it, I mean properly, like a craftsman, it's yours ...' and he cer-emoniously handed Aaron the knife. 'Only when I know you can look after it, mind. This isn't just any old knife, this is something special. It's saved my life a fair few times, I can tell you.'

Aaron remembered staring at it as it shimmered in the candlelight. It had seemed the most magical thing he had ever beheld, and even today, weighing it in his hand, it had some quality to it, something indeed special. He took two sharpening stones from the box he had had Milano prepare – with all the bits and pieces he might need for the night: polishes, needles and thread, a few basic tools and other such odds and ends – and began to carefully sharpen the blade the way Zayde had taught him. It didn't need sharpening. The knife hadn't been used to cut for over fifty years, but still each year it was sharpened and oiled and placed back in the suitcase-by-the-door.

A year after he had been given the knife Zayde died, and his father followed a month or so later. He'd never really known his father: he was a violent and uneducated man who was rarely home, usually drunk, and best avoided. All he left of any value was a gold pocket watch, and that too staked its claim in Aaron's suitcase, though he remained uncertain. Some years he put it in, for the sake of history, and family; other years he left it out, for why should he remember a father who had been no father to him? This year, he thought, he would keep it in. It wasn't big, or heavy, and he was too old for bitterness now.

Once he had finished sharpening the knife, and polishing up the watch's chased gold case, he turned his attention to an old grey woollen waistcoat and began systematically feeling for lumps along the seam, counting them as he went: 'sixty-three ... sixty-four ... sixty-five'. All there. One for every year since his father died. He was thirteen years old at the time and had a job as a sweeper at the Samuels' stone cutting workshop round the back of Brick Lane. He swept up the diamond dust and got paid by the ounce at the end of the week. Occasionally, when the cutters were working on bigger stones, a small chunk might pass unnoticed into the dust. Of course the boys were all thoroughly searched at the end of each day, and he had been brought up to be entirely honest. But then times had got harder after his father's death, more uncertain, and Mama was nervous. It had been her idea: that once a year, in the run up to Pulkhan haTik, he might swallow such a chip, of reasonable size, not so large as to be missed, not so small as to get lost, and she would find it the following evening, and sew it into the seam of a waistcoat she would make for him, that he could keep in his suitcase-by-the-door. The thought of it made Aaron shiver with disgust. Poor Mama. She was so determined, so dedicated. 'Diamonds are always good currency,' she had said. 'And as long as you don't go trying to fence it off round here no one need ever notice.' She was, of course, right, no one did ever notice.

The first six lumps along the seam from the bottom buttonhole were testament to that. He felt his way along the edge once again, carefully running the seam between his middle finger and thumb. There they were, six tiny, uneven chips of diamond, little bigger than a sugar crystal, barely noticeable in the texture of the fabric. The seventh was larger, a complete stone, and the first he had bought legitimately. That was the year he became a cutter himself. Every week he had set aside ten per cent of his wages, and on the Thursday before Pulkhan haTik, he had bought the largest whitest diamond he could afford – 0.2 carat, a real beauty. He had cut it himself. And Mama had been so proud. A few weeks later she died of a stroke. When he found her in the morning she seemed to be smiling like a little girl. And she was so young. Only forty-two. He hadn't been ready.

Yes, that year had seen many changes. He had set up his own business and moved from the East End to his first proper house, in Golders Green. He wasn't rich, but he was free. And in any case, before long he was rich. He felt further along the seam, up towards the neck, for the twenty-second stone. He didn't need to count; it was obvious if you were looking for it: a 1.5 carat emerald-cut diamond, pure white and flawless 1961, the year he made his first million, and in those days that really meant something: acceptance. He was no longer a mere diamond dealer, he was an importer, a magnate. He could make appointments to see members of the government. He was invited to dinner when the queen entertained heads of industry. And then, five years later, there it is, the biggest stone of all, 3.1 carat: a wonderful oval-cut flawless pink stone – the year he had received the royal warrant – 'Diamond Importer by Appointment to Her Majesty the Queen'. The plaque still hung above the door of his New Bond Street showroom, or so he assumed. He hadn't actually been there for years now. It was also the year that he had his first *encounter*, a beautiful young Moroccan man. He never knew his name but remembered his face to this day. Aaron smiled at the memory. Yes, 1966 had been a good year indeed.

He felt further around the neckline, about a centimetre past the final stone, and began to carefully unpick the seam, the way Mama had taught him, cutting through each stitch individually, one, two, three, four, five. That should be all it needs. Then he took a small transparent plastic bag from his pocket and tipped the contents into his hand. He held it under the candle and gazed at its surprising golden lustre. A 1.5 carat round-cut diamond, nothing particularly special, but worth a small fortune nonetheless. He carefully pushed the stone through the gap he had made in the seam and sewed it neatly into place, making sure it couldn't come loose, before examining his work under the candle. Not bad, the stitching was invisible, by this light anyway. Finally he pulled off his sweater and tried the waistcoat on. For many years it had been far too tight, but now – in his seventies, a frail old man – it fitted him perfectly once again, and strangely that felt something like a triumph. As he took it off, carefully folding it on the table, it occurred to him: he had no idea how much it would be worth today, he couldn't even guess, but it must be a good few million. And that caused him to wonder what might become of it all, after he was gone. He was leaving everything to his Foundation, but he wouldn't be saying anything about his suitcase-by-the-door. The contents of a man's suitcase should always remain secret, known only to the very closest of family. Not even Milano knew. In all likelihood the waistcoat, the whole suitcase come to that, would end up in some charity shop, or even on a rubbish dump, and again he smiled. Maybe it would be bought by a struggling student, or a tramp, and they might never know the extraordinary riches they carried about with them. He liked the randomness of it, somehow that felt appropriate.

He took off the waistcoat, put the watch in one of its pockets, wrapped it around the knife and placed the bundle back in the suitcase, just so. Then he poured himself another glass of schnapps. He had long forgotten the traditional blessing so said a simple 'to life's great absurdity!' and downed it in one gulp.

Okay. Boots. Zayde had always emphasised the importance of good boots. And he would have known! He'd trekked eight hundred miles across the mountains on his way to England. That had always impressed the young Aaron. Zayde had been on real adventures, proper life-and-death adventures. For most of his life Aaron had taken Zayde's advice quite literally with a pair of sturdy army boots. Then, back in the nineties he'd bought a modern pair of lightweight mountain-walking boots. They were a revelation; made his suitcase so much lighter. But now, well, even if he did have to get away he wouldn't be going far. Better to die with dignity at his age. And so a couple of years ago he had ordered a pair of Derby shoes from Edward Green of Germaine Street: beautiful hand-made shoes they were, their deep black lustre smouldering gently in the candlelight. They'd never been worn, and didn't need polishing, but tonight was Pulkhan haTik, so he lay a sheet of newspaper across the table-top, took up the brushes and little tin of wax, and set to work. It struck him that in his whole life he had rarely walked where proper boots were needed. He'd spent his life on pavements, in cars, hallways, offices: cities basically, and towns, but mainly cities. There were the occasional holidays abroad, but even they were mostly spent in cities. So yes, a fine pair of gentleman's town shoes was altogether more appropriate. And these were indeed the finest money could buy. He held them up and traced their curves with his fingertip. They were truly beautiful, a veritable masterpiece of the cobbler's art. Mama had after all taught him that a man needs more to live than mere necessity: necessity, history and luxury – that's what makes a man. And these shoes really were all three. For a moment he imagined himself struggling up some mountain pass, these fine shoes on his feet, dragging his suitcase behind him; and laughed out loud. It was a joke. He wouldn't get more than ten yards before needing a rest. And then it suddenly struck him: all those years ago at his mother's knee they had celebrated Pulkhan haTik for fear of the future. But today? Why did he still do it today? Was it to remember the past? Tradition? No, he did it for Mama, and he glanced up towards the mantelpiece where her photo sat in a plain wooden frame. He couldn't see it in the darkness, not even a silhouette, but he knew she was there, and she was smiling. He still missed her. Almost every day.

He packed the shoes carefully in the suitcase, and suddenly caught himself mumbling ... *Adonai Eloheino melekh ha-olam* ... That was all, and then it was gone. He had no idea what it meant. It had just come to him, a distant echo from his childhood, and the smallest hint of a tear pooled in his right eye. Was that sadness? He had nothing to be sad about. If ever a life were blessed it was his. And he had Milano. That was worth a lot.

So, where was he? He looked down at the table. Yes, necessity, history, luxury. It was all there in that plain wooden box that was the heart of his suitcase. He picked it up, slowly, carefully, feeling its weight, its balance, sensing its energy, like a sacred object, a relic, which is really what it was. He had nailed it shut, it must be over fifty years ago now, shortly after Mama had died. But he didn't need to open it. He could picture the contents perfectly. It had been a week or so after she had died. He was clearing out her room. She had so little, but those few things: her sewing tin, her wedding ring, a pack of playing cards with purple flowers on the back, a lock of her hair, and a family photograph taken when he was a child – him, Papa, Mama and Zayde, like a real family – so he had taken them, put them in the box. The rest of her things had been given away or burnt, except for the candlesticks. A few weeks later he had nailed it shut, to mark the start of a new journey, the one that had brought him here, to West Heath Road, and Milano. But he always kept it close, in his suitcase-by-the-door. Yes, necessity, history, luxury: Mama had known. She always knew. And he replaced the box carefully in the suitcase, silently mouthing a few words to his mother.

Now there was only one thing left: neatly folded on the table, a plain grey blanket. He put it on his lap and felt its texture with the flat of his hands. It was heavy, rough, hand-spun wool and he could feel the thickness of its weave, smell its rich, sheepy mustiness. But most of all he thought of Milano, of that first night they had spent together, lying side by side on that blanket, talking, touching hands, feeling close, as the sun rose over the distant mountains, flooding the room with orange-perfumed light. He remembered how the light had caught Milano's hair, how it highlighted the handsome dignity of his face, recasting him as a mythic Pasha, draping him in gold. That had been their beginning. He was under no illusions though, he knew why Milano stayed, but there was more to it than that. And in any case, he didn't believe in love. Not really. Not anymore. But companionship, and loyalty: they were real; they were to be valued.

As he pressed the blanket into the suitcase and closed the lid he found himself wondering: did he love Milano? He couldn't imagine life without him, and perhaps that was after all a kind of love.

———

It was some time before he dragged the suitcase back to its wardrobe. Somehow it always felt so much heavier at the end, as if each new diamond carried with it the weight of his conscience. There was much that he wasn't proud of, that he might have done differently had Mama lived. But when he returned to the sofa and switched on the lights her photograph smiled down at him, and he knew that she, at least, would have been proud, and that was enough; that was all that really mattered.

# All Hail Zigg

Ak-ak-ak-ak-ak-ak-ak-ak-ak-ak-ak-ak-ak

Pioew ... pioew ...

Ak-ak-ak-ak-ak-ak-ak-ak-ak-ak-ak-ak-ak-ak-ak-ak-ak-ak-ak-ak-ak-ak

Bullets ricocheted down the alley, pinging off high brick walls and garage doors into the distance.

Pioew ... pioew pioew pioew...

David ran for cover behind two large metal dustbins, but Avi was already up and waiting.

Ak-ak-ak-ak-ak-ak-ak-ak-ak-ak-ak-ak-ak-ak-ak-ak ... Ak-ak-ak-ak-ak-ak-ak-ak-ak-ak-ak-ak-ak-ak-ak-ak-ak-ak-ak-ak-ak-ak

With that final burst of fire David collapsed onto the dusty concrete clutching at his head and chest. Once down he went into epileptic spasms, before stiffening, letting out one last gargled cry, and it was over.

Avi grinned with exaggerated malevolence. He walked towards the belatedly twitching body, and gave it a gentle kick.

'Ha! Yeeddisher peeg!'

But just as he was cocking his sea-captain's peaked cap in triumph, David pulled a machine gun from his jacket pocket.

Trrrrrrrrrrrrrrrrrrrrrrrrrrrrrrrrrrrrrrrrrrrrrrrrrrrrrrrrrrrrrrrrrrrrrrrrrrrrrrrr ...

'Astalavista baby!' David did a defiant gesture with his fist, then blew the smoke from the barrel. He was a small lad for his age, scrawny, with olive skin and a face that said he was keen to please.

'You ain't got no sub-machine gun.' Avi was pissed off.

'Have too.'

'Don't be stupid. Jews didn't have guns anyway. That's what Mr K. said.'

'So ... I found it, when I fell down. Next to the body of one of your Nazi mates.'

'That's not fair.'

David stood up, and brushed the dust off his backside. 'Let me be the Nazi then'

'No, it's my hat!' Avi's expression stiffened, tightening over his pudgy cheeks, and unconsciously pouting a little around the lips. 'Anyway, I've got blue eyes, and Nazis have to have blue eyes, and anyway I'm the tallest.'

'So what!? And anyway you're the one that's moving to Israel. That makes you more Jewish than me!'

Anger flashed across Avi's face and he shoved David backwards.

David stood his ground.

'Come on then. I could take you, easy!'

The two of them puffed themselves up and stepped into each other's space. David was a good head shorter than Avi so he pulled a really angry expression to make up the difference.

'Come on then ...'

'Come on then ...'

'You first ...'

By now they were right in each other's faces, and stayed there for a few seconds, grunting at each other, before David backed down.

'Nerr, I'm bored anyway. Let's go down the Clocktower.'

And with that they bundled each other back and forth, cheerfully bickering for the sake of it, heading towards the High Street. As they approached the viaduct they heard music; a busker was playing the violin, and they took the time to dance around in front of him, leaping about ever more stupidly until he finally stopped playing and shouted at them to get lost, giving them a good excuse to run away.

Their next stop was Gelatini's ice cream parlour, where they got a double scoop each, which Avi paid for. Avi always paid for things. He got £25 a week pocket money, and his Dad drove a Ferrari. His Dad was some kind of international businessman, from Israel. He even had a yacht! Once, when they were alone at Avi's house, he had shown David his father's secret stash of gold; hidden at the back of a cupboard, an old leather bag filled with George III gold sovereigns, fifty three of them, and twelve mini gold bars like you see in heist films, only much smaller.

There was also a little velvet bag with what seemed like hundreds of sparkling diamonds, rubies and emeralds. It was amazing, proper treasure; the most exciting thing David had ever seen in all his eight and three quarter years. His Dad drove a second-hand Ford Escort and it urked him, particularly because Avi always got to choose where they'd go or what they'd have. If David ever pushed for anything Avi had the perfect put-down: *Why, are you paying?*

Half way up the High Street they settled on their usual bench to finish off the ice creams.

'I'll give you a fiver if you crush that over your head.' Avi grinned at the idea.

'Really?' David tried to hide his excitement at the thought. Five pounds was a lot of money. But he knew Avi knew that. They had done this before, and he wasn't going to be bought so easily this time.

'Sure, you've got to smear it all over your face though.'

David thought for a moment.

'Nerr, 'tsnot worth it.'

'Tenner then,' Avi responded without pause.

David thought about it again, harder this time.

'Alright then. Gimme the money first.'

Avi pulled a crinkled bunch of notes from his back pocket and gave David a tenner. Once he had safely tucked it away David duly crunched the remains of his ice cream cone over his head and smeared the crumbs and remaining chocolate contents around his face, making much play of the action. Then they both had a good laugh.

It was Saturday lunch time and half the shops were closed for the Sabbath, but the street was still fairly busy. Even so, nobody paid their larking any particular attention; just the odd glance, and that was part of the point anyway.

As they bantered away the next few minutes the scene around them began to change. Something somewhere had ended, and Orthodox Jews were suddenly everywhere: grey-bearded men in long black gabardine coats with white tassels hanging loose from their waists and wide brimmed hats, some in tall fur hats despite the heat of the day, all with white shirts and navy blue ties; women in long cover-all nylon dresses, garishly patterned with large gold plastic buttons, and discordant bows around their waists, all in the same style of straight-haired brown wig, just off the shoulders, and little uniformed children in tow, the boys in nylon navy blue suits and ties, tassels hanging loose as with the men, short cropped hair balancing mini hats that looked like drinks coasters and long curled locks hanging down beside their ears; the girls in dark pinafore dresses and high-necked white frilly blouses; and all of them, even the children, looking very serious and high minded as they meandered down the High Street in little groups.

Neither David nor Avi had ever really noticed them before. Of course they had seen them, they often appeared on the High Street at certain regular times of the week but they had never paid them any attention. But this week had been Holocaust Week, and Mr K. had shown them lots of pictures of people that looked just like these Jews here today, maybe a little grubbier but pretty much the same. He had also shown them pictures of Nazi soldiers in their smart uniforms carrying big guns and looking mean and tough. Avi's captain's hat was a pretty close match to the SS caps, who were the coolest of all. When he'd got home that day he'd written SS with a silver glitter pen on a piece of black card and stuck it in the front band, though he took it out when his parents were around.

And then on Thursday morning Mrs Freitag had come into school and talked to them for hours in an almost incomprehensible accent about what had happened to her parents, whilst they sat awkwardly cross-legged around her, and had been shouted at if they fidgeted. But in the afternoon they were rewarded with a film about a girl living in an attic, which was fairly boring but better than reading. David and Avi had got into trouble for giggling at one point and were sent to sit at opposite corners of the room, and then it got even more boring. They hadn't understood the ending.

When asked if anyone in the class was Jewish almost half had put their hands up, including David and Avi, but none of them looked like these Jews here. They were normal people. These Jews were weirdoes.

'My Dad says that they're the ones that make all the trouble in Israel.'

'Really?' David was surprised. Sure, they looked like weirdoes, but not trouble-makers.

'He says they're all fanatics. And most of them come from America. He says they build houses in the desert to annoy the Arabs. That's why we're going back. He says where there's trouble there's money to make.'

'They don't sound American.'

'Yeah, I know.'

There was a pregnant pause whilst they both considered this.

'I dare you to shoot them!' David grinned through his chocolate-smeared face.

'What?'

'Go on ... I dare you.'

'Why me? You do it.'

'No, it's your hat. Or are you chicken.' David made the chicken noise that couldn't be refused as a point of honour. 'Burrrrp brp brp brp brp burrrrp brp brp brp.'

'Alright then.' Avi didn't usually take up dares, but after David's heroic display earlier he didn't want to be left out.

The two of them sat there in anticipation as a group of men, old and young, bearded, side-locked and each clutching books sealed in see-through plastic covers, headed their way. Once they had just passed Avi jumped up on the bench and pointed his imaginary machine gun.

Ak-ak-ak-ak-ak-ak-ak-ak-ak-ak-ak-ak-ak-ak-ak-ak-ak-ak-ak-ak-ak-ak-ak.

The Jews paid them no attention whatever.

'That was rubbish. You gotta jump out in front of them.'

'Why? That wasn't the deal.'

'They're not going to die if they don't even notice you.'

David imagined the Jews joining in their game, clutching at their chests and falling to the floor.

'You do it then. Or are you ch ch ch ch ch chikeeeen ...'

'Alright, gimme the hat then.'

'No way, hoesay, you'll get chocolate all over it.'

'I'm not doing it without the hat.'

'Ch ch ch ch ch ch chikeeen chikeen ...'

'Alright, alright. Watch this then.'

A group of three Jewish women were heading their way. One was old; the other two were pushing prams and had a neatly managed group of four young boys and two young girls at their side. The women were engaged in quiet discussion.

David jumped out in front of them and emptied two magazines of machine-gun rounds into the group.

Trrrrrrrrrrrrrrrrrrrrrrrrrrrrrrrrrrrrrrrrrrrrrrrrrrrrrrrrrrrrrrrrrrrrr ... Trrrrrrrrrrr
rrrrrrrrrrrrrrrrrrrrrrrrrrrrrrrrrrrrrrrrrrrrrrrrrrrrrrrrrrrrrrrr ...

Again they paid no attention whatever, politely walking around him
as they passed, even the children. When he hopped back onto the bench
Avi was laughing.

'You looked like a twat!'

'What about you in your stupid hat!' With that David punched Avi
on the arm as hard as he could. For a moment Avi was shocked, he had
been caught by surprise, but quickly responded with a kick to David's
shin.

'Owww. That hurt!'

Then they both laughed as David wiped his hand over his sticky chocolate hair and smeared it across Avi's face. Avi shoved him again.

'What was it the Nazis all shouted in that film?' David asked once
they had calmed down.

'Hail something, I think,' Avi replied.

'Hail Zigg! That was it. All hail Zigg' A look of triumph crossed
David's grubby face.

'Who was Zigg anyway?'

'I don't know. Must have been a nickname for Hitler.'

'Anyway, why?' asked Avi, who was never one to consider schoolwork
after hours.

'Maybe if we both jump out and do that salute thing and shout All
Hail Zigg ... Then they might not ignore us.'

'Okay then, together mind.'

'Sure.'

They looked around. A group of old men in long grey beards and
broad fur hats was heading their way.

'After three ...' said David.

'One ...'

'Two ...'

'Three,' and they both jumped over the back of the bench into the
path of the Jewish Elders, and raised their arms in a Nazi salute.

'All hail Zigg! All hail Zigg!' David started and Avi joined in.

'All hail Zigg! All hail Zigg! All hail Zigg! All hail Zigg! All hail Zigg!
All hail Zigg!'

Still not a single response. It was as if they just weren't there. Once the Jews had passed them without casting a single backward glance their way, they stopped saluting and climbed back onto the bench despondently.

'They're freaks!'

David remained silent. He was thinking *no wonder the Nazis wanted to get them*, but knew that was a bad thing to think and so tried to stop himself.

'Didn't Mr K. say that the women all wear wigs, and shave their heads?' Avi continued.

'Yeah,' replied David. His tone was noncommittal. He knew something was coming.

'Well I dare you to pull one of their wigs off.'

'No way!'

Avi reached into his pocket and pulled out another note.

'I dare you a tenner.' He waved it in David's face.

Twenty pounds. David had never had so much money – he could buy those binoculars he'd been looking at in Dixons. But then he knew it was a step too far. But then again, these people weren't normal, they would probably just ignore him anyway. And so far they'd just been making fools out of the two of them. After less thought than he'd intended he snatched the tenner from Avi.

'Alright, you're on.'

They looked around.

'Look there's one. That definitely looks like a wig.' Avi was pointing at a youngish woman pushing a pram, with a short bearded man wearing a trilby at her side. The woman's hair was shoulder length and didn't quite look real. They were on the other side of the road.

'Just grab it and run off. I'll be right behind you. We'll head for the alley.'

'Alright.' David still wasn't sure about it, but it was too late to back down, and the twenty pounds felt good in his pocket.

Suddenly, before he really knew it he was running across the road towards the family. As he reached them he leapt up and grabbed the woman's hair but it didn't come right off and instead yanked her to the side, pulling her around and knocking over the pram. The woman screamed, and the baby screamed but David's hand was still caught in the wig which was half over the woman's face, and he couldn't get away quickly enough. Then the man grabbed him by the arm and starting shouting at him: *What the fuck are you doing! You little fucker!* He slapped David hard around the face, twice, and carried on shouting. Finally David's hand came free of the wig but he was still firmly gripped by the man. The woman and baby were still screaming and the man was still shouting. David tried slipping his jacket off, but the grip was too tight. Then Avi appeared and laid a massive punch square on the man's nose, but even that didn't loosen his grip. Finally Avi kicked the man in the balls, and as he fell to the floor David wriggled free and the two of them ran for their lives before hiding behind a parked car about a hundred yards down the road.

Avi was laughing hysterically. David was crying.

'Don't be such a baby. We got away with it, didn't we.'

David didn't feel like a baby. He felt ashamed, but couldn't admit that to Avi so dried his eyes. His cheeks were bright red and stung horribly. But he knew he deserved it.

They peered through the back window of the car to see if anyone was following them. A small crowd had gathered around the couple but no one was coming their way. They could still hear the woman screaming and the man shouting, all now at a safe distance.

'Did you see her face!' Avi was still laughing. 'And anyway her head wasn't bald. Mr K. was wrong, more like a number four.' He said that with some satisfaction. Then suddenly he stopped laughing. 'Damn, my hat. It must have fallen off.'

'Why don't you go back and get it.' David said sarcastically. He was angry at Avi for getting him into this.

'Nerr, Mum will buy me a new one. I'll tell her one of the bigger boys stole it.' David didn't doubt it. He's seen Avi put on a show of righteous upset to his Mum before, and always seemed to get his own way.

They stayed hidden behind the car for around five minutes until the street had returned to normal, then headed back towards the alley and their respective houses. Avi wanted to stay out a bit longer but David was keen to get home. As they parted company on Woodville Road Avi repeatedly shot David in the back with his machine gun, but got no response. Then he headed off to the garages and his secret hideout.

David didn't tell anyone what had happened. He went straight up to his room, threw the twenty pounds in his bin and lay on the bed trying not to cry. He stayed there for what felt like hours until his mother shouted him for Dr Who.

Later, at bedtime, he retrieved the money and hid it carefully under his mattress. At least he could get those binoculars now, which made him feel a little better.

—

Avi couldn't get to sleep that night. He was thinking about Israel! His parents called it home, even though his Mum was English, but to him it was a faraway land. He'd been just six months old when they left, and they'd never gone back. His Mum said it was very like Golders Green, but the trees hang with oranges and lemons, and the sun always shines. Sometimes, she said, on summer evenings great flocks of giant bats descend on the streets to eat the fruit, swooping and swirling into the sky like little black puffs of cloud. But Avi wasn't sure he believed her. That sounded like the kind of thing mums tell you to make you think it's all going to be great. He wasn't six any more.

Aba, Avi's father, didn't talk much about Israel. He didn't talk much about much. Avi knew he'd been in the Israeli army, everyone joins the army, even girls! And he grew up in a town called Bnei Brak, near a city called Tel Aviv which has a long sandy beach and palm trees. That was where they were going to live, a short walk from the beach front. But other than that Aba really only talked to him about sport and home-work. Sometimes Avi heard him talking to his Mum about the *dosim*, the crazy religious Jews who lived in the desert and were always causing trouble; and the Arabs, who were the enemy of the Jews, though his parents often seemed to take their side, which confused him. These con-versations were conducted in Hebrew, and everyone pretended that he didn't understand, but he did.

All he really knew was that he didn't want to go. Israel may be *their* home, but his home was right here, in Golders Green, England, with his friends. Yoni, who had moved from Israel a year ago, said that Israeli schools were really strict, and they didn't even play football. And then there was the language. He didn't like Hebrew. Sure, he could speak it, or at least understand it; but he knew it as the language his Dad fell into whenever he was angry; an aggressive language that was shouted. He'd been going to Hebrew lessons for the last six months, 'to catch up with his new schoolmates' as his mother put it, but he found it hard, particularly the writing. So no, he didn't want to go to Israel. He was scared, and he was angry, really angry.

All these thoughts whirled around his head as he lay there, tangling the blankets, tossing this way and that. It wasn't fair! How dare they take him away! They didn't have the right.

Once he could hear his parents quietly snoring next door, he turned on his bedside light and crept across the room to his secret hiding place. He squeezed his arm into the gap under the wardrobe, where he knew his mother's fat arm couldn't reach, and stretched towards the back, feeling for something soft. Then triumph flashed across his face as he withdraw his hand, clutching an old grey school sock. He climbed back onto his bed and tipped the contents out into his hand: two George III gold sovereigns. He didn't know what they were worth, but it had to be a lot; they were solid gold, so Aba said. And it wasn't really stealing. Aba had called it the family's treasure, *just in case*; so a third of it was his anyway.

He lay down in the bed and pulled the covers up to his neck, still clutching the two coins in his hand. The weight was comforting, as he knew it meant value. Gold was valued by the gramme, and they were by far the heaviest coins he had ever held. If he decided to run away they should keep him going for a fair while. He could live in his hideout, in the garages under the train track, hardly anyone went there. He could hold out for weeks, and they can't take him away if they can't find him.

He lay there for some time, imagining his life as an outlaw, soon becoming a kind of pirate, with a crew of rough-and-ready shipmates loyal to his every command, and before he realised it had happened, he was asleep.

# A Fool Will Stay a Fool

Simon was stunned, though the businessman in him ensured he didn't show it. He turned the pocket watch over in his hand and opened the back. *Compensateur et parachute – Breguet no.2654.* Unbelievable! Just three numbers off. It was obviously stolen; no question, and normally he wouldn't even consider buying stolen goods. But he had to have this watch. It was fate; God's will. He opened the inner case to examine the mechanism, making a show of adjusting his magnifier, and peering intently. It was clear why it didn't work; a simple case of a loose spring: it had been over-wound. The rest of the mechanism looked in near perfect condition. It was wonderful craftsmanship, a very fine piece of work. But most of all, it was just what he needed, what he'd almost given up hope of ever finding. And it had been brought to him! To his workshop! And at what would no doubt be a bargain price! Silently he said a short prayer to thank the Lord for granting him this moment, then looked up at the young man across the counter. He was fairly tall, lanky, with short cropped hair and rather large ears. There was something slightly stupid about his face, possibly a little thuggish. He wore a black hoody with a skull printed in white on the front, and his baggy jeans were hung so low you could see a large band of bright red underpants around his waist. He obviously had no idea what he had in his possession.

'So mate, what do you reckon?'

Simon closed the watch and placed it on the counter. 'Well, the mechanism is completely jammed; one of the screws may have come loose. The repeater hammer is missing, the spring is broken, and the cylinder escapement needs replacing. But I suspect worse. I won't know until I take it apart, but ... Have you taken it to anyone else?'

'No.'

'Well it looks like someone has made a hash of trying to repair it, and

51

there may even be a couple of wheels missing. As I say, I won't know for sure until I examine it properly.'

'So how much do you reckon?' The young man was shifting his weight from one leg to the other.

'What do you say I give you two hundred for it?'

'Come on, mate, that's gold, and it's pretty old. It's gotta be worth more than that.'

'If it were working, sure. But as it is? Can I sell a broken watch? I may have to make new parts for it, by hand, and that is time-consuming work, very fiddly, and my eyes are not what they were. Maybe for me it is not worth it. Now if you leave it with me, then I could take a proper look, then I could tell you for sure. But as it is ...?' This was a gamble, but he had a hunch the young man would want a quick and easy sale. He twisted the tip of his beard in a masquerade of deep consideration. 'Okay, and God knows I'm a fool, say, two hundred and fifty? And I'm doing you a favour.'

'Alright, it's a deal. Cash, mind?'

'But of course.' He reached down behind the counter for a metal box which he opened with a key and counted out five fifty-pound notes. Then he took out his ledger and pulled a pen from his jacket pocket.

'Two hundred and fifty pounds.' He spoke the words out loud as his wrote. 'Breguet gold-cased pocket watch. Broken. And your name is?'

'Call me Pete.'

'Surname?'

'Just Pete.'

'And your address?'

'I'm not giving you my fucking address, mate. Make something up ...' He took the money from the counter and walked to the door, then turned back to Simon and pointed at him, raising his eyebrows in a mildly threatening manner. 'Seeing ya ...'

Well, £250 for an 1811 Bregeut quarter pump repeater, and in near perfect condition. It's got to be worth at least ten grand, a real museum piece. But that wasn't the point. He went into the back office, opened the safe, and removed a small black leather pouch. Once back at the counter he took from it a gold pocket watch, his family pocket watch passed down through at least six generations. He placed it next to his new acquisition. They were identical. He turned them over, opened them up, and examined the mechanisms under the magnifier. Yes, a perfect match, numbers 2654 and 2651, the exact same model, made at the same time in the same workshop. He leant back in his chair, stroking his beard. He finally had it, in his hands; he had given up hope years ago, stopped even looking. But here it was. A gift.

He had told the story a thousand times; why he became a watchmaker: 'You see my father; he was this great engineer, a boy genius no less. And so it happened that at the age of ten, when left alone one evening, he took the family pocket watch and dismantled it, piece by piece, to see how it worked, you understand. When he was discovered there was nothing but a pile of cogs and springs and wheels. Now after the customary beating he insisted he could put it back together. And that he did. If anything it kept time better than before. So I, at the age of ten, I wanted to be like my father, so one evening, when I was left alone, I took the pocket watch and my father's tools, and I took it apart, completely apart. But all I could see was a pile of cogs and springs and wheels that made no sense at all. And then nobody could put it back together, not even my father, not even the finest craftsmen in London. And so I became a watchmaker. Perhaps I am still seeking my father's approval, God forgive him.' But now, now he had the parts, original parts, the cogs and screws that had been lost, the ruby cylinder escapement, all in perfect working condition. It had to be God's will.

At that moment the workshop came alive with a cacophony of chimes. It was three o'clock; Shabbos was calling. He gathered up the two watches and placed them both carefully in the safe. Just as he was locking up a lone cuckoo clock announced its own inaccuracy. Hmm ... so it was still running slow. One day, he thought, one day they would all come alive at the very same moment. *And one day the Moshiach will come and the sick will all be healed ...* Ah, but a fool will stay a fool. And he smiled to himself.

That evening he told his wife with great enthusiasm all about the watch, how it must be a gift from God, and she nodded dutifully, whilst preparing the cholent, and wondering which scarf she should wear to shul. Clocks and watches. It was all he ever talked about. For thirty years she'd heard nothing but clocks and watches. And indeed, it was all he could think about: throughout the Sabbath meal; listening to his wife go on at length about Mrs Levine's new conservatory; as he sat in the synagogue; even talking to Rabbi Feldman about his cousin's business: in his mind all he saw was the gold pocket watch, and he rehearsed over and over what he was to do to make it whole again. Never had he been so impatient for the Shabbos to end.

———

As soon as the Havdalah candle was extinguished he put on his coat, made an excuse to his wife, who smiled but barely noticed, and returned, at last, to his workshop. He switched on the lights just as his many clocks, cluttering on every surface and wall space, all chimed into life, as if to greet him. It was nine o'clock. He probably had a couple of hours left in his old eyes.

He retrieved the two watches and placed them on his workbench. It was a shame in a way; such a beautiful piece, and in near perfect condition. But it had to be. It was meant to be. Just then the cuckoo clock whirred as the little bird ventured forth. Three more minutes in only twenty-four hours. That was more than just a simple adjustment to the nut. He would probably have to shorten the suspension arm by another two millimetres. But that was not for now.

He pulled the magnifier into place and began the meticulous task of dismantling the watch, piece by piece, carefully checking each part for wear before dropping it into an old tobacco tin. He had no need to take the usual notes regarding order and placement; he knew the workings of this model intimately, even the parts he had never knowingly seen before, the parts that had been missing since he was a boy. Many times over the years he had planned to make replacements himself, studying the published drawings, even making a few dummies in cheap brass, but something had always prevented him from completing the task. In the end he had decided he needed original parts, made in the Breguet workshop, parts he was never likely to find: parts like these. Three times his many clocks announced the hour before the final piece was dropped into the tin and the gold case lay empty on his workbench.

By the time he got home his wife's snores were rattling china in the kitchen and so he chose to sleep on the sofa, at the opposite end of the house. That night he dreamt that he had died, and his whole life had flashed before him. He woke up, strangely jarred, to the sound of women gossiping in the hallway. Then the front door closed behind them, and silence, except for the gentle ticking of a number of clocks about the house. His wife insisted that the bells were all switched off. They disturbed her peace. In truth, Simon suspected that she didn't really like clocks. To her they were just a means of measuring time; a digital watch would do just as well, and far more quietly. He lay there, on the sofa, for a surprising amount of time, listening to the ticking, thinking about his dream, about the pocket watch, about the stiffness in his neck from lying crooked all night.

He arrived back at the workshop just after eleven. As he looked in the tin there was a touch of regret at what he had done, but it soon passed as he turned his thoughts to the other watch, his family watch; a watch that would soon tick again for the first time in over fifty years.

This was much more fiddly work. It was always easier to take things apart than put them back together. Slowly, carefully, he set about the task: first removing the verge and the main ratchet ensemble; fitting the new ratchet wheel; replacing the cracked cylinder escapement, the click-spring and the missing second wheel; then painstakingly reassembling the various parts to make the mechanism whole once again. Lastly he realigned and pinned the fusee in preparation for fitting the spring, the final piece, the heart that would bring it life. He picked it up with his crooked tweezers and held it under the magnifier. Along the side he could read the name, *Breguet*.

And then it struck him: this was an important moment, a culmination, and not something to be undertaken lightly. He dropped the spring in the tin and leant back in his chair, deep in thought, remembering his dream. Had not his whole life been defined by the breaking of this watch? His choice of profession; hence where he had studied, where he set up his little shop; the people he had met; his wife, she had been a customer; and his friends: and yet every time he had thought to fix it, something had stopped him. But now, now it was real, a two-minute job and it would all be over. The watch would be ticking once again, chiming every quarter, as his father had known it. Maybe he would wait a little; maybe he wasn't yet quite ready for that. And really, it was time he headed home. He placed the spring carefully in a small brown envelope and slipped it into his waistcoat pocket.

—

The following Shabbos Simon arrived home as usual; idly chatted to his wife as she prepared the food, as usual; said the many blessings, ate and drank, all as usual. Then, after dinner, as they settled down in the front room to read he unexpectedly broke the silence.

'I have a gift for you,' he said, took from his pocket a blue velvet presentation box and handed it to her. She opened it to find a small gold brooch, with golden leaves around the edge, and at its centre, behind glass, a tiny blue spiral watch spring.

As he explained to her what it was, its importance, why he hadn't fitted it, and how he had got his cousin, a jeweller, to mount it in crystal and gold, she nodded dutifully, as always, but inside her heart had cracked, for now the silence was broken, a silence that had lasted for longer than she could remember, she would have to speak. She looked down at the locket, then back at Simon.

'I can't take this,' she said, passing the locket back to her husband, and then started to weep, gently at first, but soon falling into great rolling sobs. Simon was stunned, and didn't know what he should do. He hadn't seen her cry in many years, and, truth to tell, had spent much of his life avoiding emotional situations. People, he had often thought, are not like clocks. When a clock is upset you can open it up, take it apart, work out what is wrong, then set about fixing it. But people, they baffled him with their unpredictability and messy complications. So he just sat there, for what felt like hours, listening to her sobs, feeling a tightness and a distance rising inside him. Finally he stood to try to comfort her, but she brushed him away, then ran upstairs to her bedroom saying 'I'm sorry, I'm so sorry' through her tears.

And then he was alone.

He looked at the locket, admiring its fine workmanship and symbolic potency, then placed it on the coffee table and leant back in his chair. He could feel an anxiety at his wife's response growing inside him, but managed to stifle it, as he always did, and returned to reading his book. No doubt she would come down soon and explain, and then everything would be fine again. But she didn't come down, and so he decided it was probably best to sleep on the sofa.

—

The following morning, after a sound and dreamless sleep, Simon went into the kitchen to find his wife sat at the breakfast table. She seemed pale, smaller than usual, and her eyes were a little red. She looked up at him without smiling, as if some great weight were upon her.

'I'm leaving you,' she said, her expression barely changing.

Simon just looked at her blankly.

'I don't love you anymore,' she continued. 'I don't think I have for some time now, and if you were honest I think you would know you don't love me either.'

He noticed the suitcase at her side.

'Where will you go?' he asked, his voice expressing no emotion, though she thought she saw a fleeting sadness in his eyes.

'I have a friend,' she replied. 'He will take care of me.'

There was a long silence, and they looked at each other, neither saying what they were really thinking.

'I'll come back in a week or so,' she said finally, 'to sort out my things.' Then she stood up.

He continued to watch her blankly as she picked up her suitcase and headed towards the front door, then turned back towards him.

'Will you be alright?' she asked with an unexpected kindness he hadn't heard from her in years.

'Of course,' he replied, not knowing what else to say.

And then she left, quietly closing the door behind her.

Simon stood there for a minute or so, then poured himself a coffee from the percolator his wife had prepared and continued with his day as if nothing unusual had happened. And anyway, he felt sure she would be back. She always was.

—

When he got home from his workshop that evening he went around the house switching on the chimes of his many clocks, made himself a hot salt beef sandwich and sat on the sofa to eat. At eight o'clock the whole house came alive in a unison he had longed to hear for many years. As he had suspected it was only the grandfather clock in the hallway that was out by a couple of seconds. He would have adjusted it long ago but his wife objected to him tinkering in the house: 'That's why you've got a workshop,' she would say, with that adamant look of hers that invited no answer. But now, whilst she was gone, he could do as he wished, and so took a screwdriver from the kitchen drawer and made the adjustment, which only took a minute.

Later that evening, sitting on the edge of his bed in his long blue striped nightshirt, his beard neatly cupped in a hairnet pulled up around his ears, he took the watch from the bedside table and carefully, with all the delicacy of a master's hand, began to wind it, feeling for every little click along the way. And then, as if by magic, its little heart was beating once again and it seemed to him that the whole world was a better place for it.

As he lay in bed, listening to the comforting sound of its gentle tick, he thought about how something had been broken, and another thing had been mended, and wasn't that the way of things after all.

# The Miraculous Rabbi Feldman

As Rabbi Feldman stepped into his bathroom to conduct his bedtime ablutions that Sunday evening he had no idea of the events that were about to unfold. Indeed had he the smallest of inklings he most likely would have retained his underpants, for as he stood at the sink, brushing his teeth, dressed only as God Above had made him, he cast a last casual glance through the window at the comforting silhouette of his synagogue across the road, as was his habit, only to be horrified by a dimly flickering orange glow behind the stained glass, and the sudden flash of a torch beam.

'Vandals!' The shout was a reflex. 'Vandals in the synagogue!' He burst into the bedroom, where Mrs Feldman was reading. 'Vandals in the synagogue! Call the police! Call the fire brigade! Vandals!'

What happened next was to surprise everyone, for Rabbi Feldman had never been a brave man, nor really a popular man, nor had he ever done anything remark-worthy in his entire life. But on this occasion, seeing his synagogue under threat, the synagogue his great-grandfather had built, that his grandfather and father had presided over before him; well, something snapped inside, something that had never snapped before, probably would never snap again, and, with an almighty roar, he grabbed the first garment that came to hand, which happened to be his prayer shawl, flung it over his shoulders and ran from the house, shouting all the while: 'Vandals! Vandals in the synagogue! Call the police!' When asked later why he had taken his tallis, and not, say, a coat, or anything else more concealing, he would raise his finger in imitation of the wise and declare: 'if ever a man should be prepared to meet his maker it is when confronting vandals in the synagogue.' And though he knew that not to be the real answer, he was never quite sure what was. It was one of many things he would ponder in the months to come.

By the time he reached the side door to the synagogue, a mere fifty yards across the road, he had already lost much of his bluster, and seeing it had been forced further stole the wind from his sails, but the smell of smoke, and the thought of rising flames inside spurred him onwards nonetheless. He quickly made his way down the corridor to the main Sanctuary. Smoke was billowing above him, and ahead, through the glass doors, the tell-tale flickering orange light of flames. He grabbed a fire extinguisher from the wall and ran into the hall.

It wasn't as bad as he had feared; a pile of prayer books and a couple of broken wooden chairs in the middle of the centre aisle. The flames had barely taken hold and a few bursts of foam was all it took to put them out. Looking around it seemed that the damage was fairly minimal, though his eyes were still adjusting to the darkness. The smoke had risen to the ceiling, which would probably need a repaint, and obviously the aisle carpet was ruined, but the insurance should cover it all.

Suddenly he was blinded by a bright light in his face.

'And who the fuck do we have here then? A naked fatty with a shrivelled dick.' It was a young male voice, a thug's voice. Again instinct took over, though not at all the instinct he expected, the one that would have told him to run. No, this was a different and quite surprising instinct, the instinct to pray, to say Kaddish, and he walked towards the light, reciting the words – *Yisgaddal veyisqaddash shmeh rabboh'* – raised the fire extinguisher high above his head – *Be'olmo' di vro' khir'useh* – and threw it, with every ounce of his remaining strength, towards the blinding whiteness. There was an almighty crash, a stifled shriek of pain and then the sound of something soft but heavy slumping to the floor.

If only the police had arrived at that moment Rabbi Feldman might have concluded the evening's adventure with some semblance of dignity, but, alas for him, that was not to be, for Jonny was upstairs, searching cupboards for valuables, and Jonny was not such a pushover as Squint – he had more to prove, and now he had a gun to prove it with. However, the sight that greeted him as he re-entered the hall was so unexpected, so entirely astonishing that even Jonny felt a thrill of fear chill his blood, if only for a moment. There, standing over the body of his mate was a short, fat, naked man, with a white shawl draped over his shoulders, muttering to himself in some weird foreign language, like a scene straight out of a horror film. Jonny pulled out his gun.

'Shut the fuck up! You just shut the fuck up!'

But Rabbi Feldman couldn't help himself. Seeing the gun pointed at him, and the body lying at his feet, he was paralysed with fear and his mouth just kept on moving.

'SHUT IT!' Jonny pointed the gun at the ceiling and pulled the trigger. It was the loudest sound Rabbi Feldman had ever heard and succeeded in shaking him from his paralysis. He collapsed onto his knees and began to beg for his life.

'What've you done to Squint?! What've you fucking done to him?!' The gun was now pointed squarely at the rabbi's head, and not more than a foot away.

'I'm going to fucking kill you, you mental motherfucker!'

Stricken with terror as he was, time seemed to run more slowly for the rabbi, and in those few seconds he offered up the contents of the safe, all the synagogue silver, and even the keys to his Mercedes, but to no avail, for Jonny had seen the red mist, and once that had happened nothing would stop him, except, of course, divine intervention. Jonny leant forward and pressed the gun against the rabbi's forehead. He raised his eyebrows as if this were just a game, then pulled the trigger. There was a click, Rabbi Feldman shat himself, but no bang.

'What the ...' Jonny raised the gun and re-cocked it. 'Hold on a minute mate, the fucking thing's jammed.' He emptied a bullet from the barrel, replaced it, closed the barrel with a twist of his wrist, and held it again at the Rabbi's forehead.

Another click.

'I'm real sorry about this, mate.'

The rabbi quietly whimpered to himself.

Jonny pointed the gun at the ceiling. BANG! Small pieces of plaster rained down on them. Then once again pressed it to the rabbi's forehead. Click. Just then the air was filled with the sound of sirens heading their way. Jonny looked down at the pathetic blob of a man before him, then at Squint, who was still out cold. 'Fucking thing! ... Looks like it's your lucky day then, mate!' And he casually walked away, turning only once to add 'be seeing ya!'

When the police arrived and turned on the lights they found Rabbi Feldman, naked, his tallis around his shoulders, blubbering, in a mess of his own excrement, though in their report they politely described it as 'semi-dressed and in a state of shock'. Squint was coming around by then and was taken off in an ambulance as a precaution. Rabbi Feldman was given a coat by one of the officers, which he repeatedly promised to get dry-cleaned, and after two hours of questioning returned home where he spent the rest of the night in the bath, quietly weeping to himself and avoiding Mrs Feldman's pitying looks.

—

The rumours started immediately, even before the police had arrived, for Mrs Levine had seen the rabbi running across the street, naked and shouting as if possessed by a dybbuk, and, despite the lateness of the hour, had deemed the sight worthy of at least a few brief phone calls. Needless to say, Mrs Solomons, one of the recipients, was first in line at Klein's the following morning, having contrived to run out of bread – the birds breakfasted well that day – and soon found herself the centre of attention.

'Ruthie saw him with her very own eyes, naked as G-d made him, except for his tallis, that is – now there's piety for you. They're saying he saved the synagogue; put out the fire; tackled one vandal with his bare hands, and scared the others off; and all in his birthday suit. And they had guns. Ruthie heard at least six shots...'

By the time the bakery was closing the great rabbi had personally fended off all five of the intruders and his tallis was riddled with bullet holes and singed around the edges, though miraculously he was unharmed. That was when Mrs Feldman arrived to collect a box of coconut macaroons. She was mobbed the moment she entered the shop with a gaggle of questions and assertions from every direction.

'Ladies, ladies ... Walter is fine, just a little shaken, as well he might be.'

'How many were there?'

'I heard he knocked three of them out with his bare hands.'

'And they had guns?'

'Oh, yes, Ruthie heard the whole thing. Said it sounded like Hebron.'

'And he was naked? Why would he be naked?'

'Ladies, please.' She raised her voice like the school teacher she had once been, immediately commanding silence.

'Last night a couple of young thugs tried to set fire to the synagogue. And yes, Walter stopped them. And yes, he wasn't wearing much. He was about to get into bed when he saw the flames, and grabbed the first thing that came to hand, which happened to be his tallis.'

'Is it true his tallis has bullet holes?

'How bad is the synagogue?'

'And he was naked?'

'That's probably what scared them off.'

'Ladies, please ... The synagogue will be fine, though it will be closed for a few days as the police are investigating. They got one of them but the other got away. And what with a gun being involved ... And Walter just needs a few days rest to get over the fright ... That's all there is to it. Now, if you don't mind, I've really got to get to the post office before it closes.'

But Mrs Feldman was worried about the rabbi. He wouldn't leave the bedroom, wouldn't even open the curtains or turn on the light. He just sat there, bolt upright in his bed, staring at a crack along the far wall that looked, to him, like the Hebrew character Reysh, the symbol of Choice, Greatness or Degradation, and the wickedness of Man. He hadn't said a word since the police left, and even then he had been largely incoherent. Hopefully a plate of macaroons and a good night's sleep would bring him back to himself.

———

Nobody admitted talking to the journalists who had been noseying around all afternoon. They had come for an armed robbery in a synagogue, but a naked rabbi saves the day – well, that was more than a bonus; could even be a front page. By the time they heard about the bullet holes in the prayer shawl they were virtually drooling.

The story made page six of the *Sun*, with the headline 'Would Jew Believe It', and page nine of the *Mirror*, together with a mocked-up photograph of a bullet-holed prayer shawl to aid the imagination of its readers. Both papers seemed to have taken their accounts more from the prattling tongues of gossip-mongers than the police statement, or the synagogue's official press release. Rabbi Feldman had fought off four or five intruders respectively, wrestling them to the ground and tying them up using a box of teffilin (the *Mirror* – God forgive their ignorance) or beating them over the head with the Torah scroll (the *Sun* – such a notion is probably beyond forgiveness). Both papers did agree on one thing: his prayer shawl was singed around the edges and scarred with at least five bullet holes. The *Express* joined in the next day with a cartoon of a naked rabbi flying through the air, dodging bullets, his tallis a cape, over the caption 'Faster than a speeding bagel'.

The synagogue remained cordoned off for three days whilst a police forensic team pulled bullets from the ceiling, dusted everything for fingerprints and generally investigated. When they finally left, Mrs Feldman, who had always run her husband's affairs, busied herself organising the clean-up, sorting out the insurance claim, and arranging for various of the rabbi's students to take over his duties for the next few days, until he was back to himself. Meanwhile, the rabbi just sat, bolt upright in his bed, staring at the crack on the far wall, and didn't say a word.

By Thursday the story was being tweeted, blogged, chatted, commented and poked internationally, albeit amongst certain circles, and video reconstructions began to appear on YouTube from as far afield as Tokyo and Honduras. On Friday the story was taken up by the more hysterical Jewish newspapers around the world, and by Saturday it had made its way into mainstream international commentaries. By now the story was focused on the miraculous prayer shawl, which was being credited by some with protecting the rabbi from all harm. Rabbi Feldman himself was being compared with the great rabbis of old in the presence and strength of his faith. By the following Monday even the most serious purveyors of news had decided that the hysteria surrounding the story was worthy of a story in itself, and so Mrs Feldman found her husband's awful publicity photo from the synagogue's website on page seven of the *Guardian*, page six of the *Independent* and page nineteen of *The Times*.

Poor Rabbi Feldman remained completely unaware of the furore that was growing up around him. He stayed in his bed, in the dark, sat bolt upright, staring straight ahead at the crack on the far wall. Doctors came and went, both of the body and of the head, and each time the rabbi roused himself from his trance to politely answer their questions – yes, he was doing fine, just a little tired; no, he didn't require any medication to help him sleep; yes, he just needed a little more time – but as soon as they left he would return to his staring and thinking and questioning ...

Then, quite unexpectedly, on the morning of the tenth day, Rabbi Feldman arose from his bed, got dressed in his second finest navy blue suit, and came down for breakfast as if none of it had happened. His wife and three children, being in many ways the perfect family, took up the cue and continued as if everything were normal. They chatted and teased and mumbled and bumbled their way through breakfast, then out into the car for Mrs Feldman to drive them to their various schools.

When she returned, on seeing her husband still sat at the breakfast table she gave him a look that only a wife can give, a mixture of pity, compassion, entreaty and love, and he felt he must owe her some sort of explanation.

'You see ...' His eyes were downcast and his hands clasped tightly together in front of him on the table. 'You see, as a rabbi I often have to talk of the terrible suffering of our people, of the slaves in Egypt, a thousand years of pogroms, and the holocaust, every year the holocaust; it's part of our culture, our tradition. And so I have often thought, what if that had been me? If Death were standing before me, dressed as a Cossack or a Nazi, what kind of man would I turn out to be? And I always thought that I would be one of those standing to the end, with dignity, with pride in my faith, in my people, my culture – but now I know: I'm the man who blubbers and shits himself, who begs for his life and offers up the keys to the kingdom.'

He looked up at her imploringly, his eyes swelling and red, and she went to him, and held him in her arms. The moment he felt her touch the dam burst and he crumpled in a flood of tears, and Mrs Feldman was happy to have her Walter back.

For the rest of the day they stayed in and talked. Mrs Feldman made pots of tea and brought plates of sweet biscuits as he told her the truth of what had happened; how he had lost his courage just when it counted most; how the gun had jammed three times as it was pointed at his head. 'Perhaps it was faulty, something to do with the angle it was held at; perhaps he was just playing with me – but maybe, just maybe, I keep coming back to this, maybe the Lord was looking down and jammed the gun, but if he did, then why did he save me only to humiliate me? and why did I grab my tallis? Why not a coat? And why say Kaddish? It makes no sense to me, as if I were acting someone else's script. But maybe that's how it is when haShem is present.' And Mrs Feldman listened as only a good wife can, allowing him his dignity, his space, occasionally squeezing his knee for reassurance. Once he was spent she told him all about the hoo-ha that had arisen over his tallis; showed him the many newspaper clippings she had collected; told him how the synagogue had to call the police when a large crowd of Jews for Jesus had gathered wanting to see the miraculous tallis. 'It's funny,' she said, trying to make him smile, 'the effect that Jesus has, even Jews, when they are for him, they go mad ... Speaking of which, the Chabad wants to talk to you ...'

Later that evening as he sat around the table with his wife and three children playing Trivial Pursuit, deliberately losing to give Izzy, age seven, a chance, it struck him that he did have much to be grateful for. But all the while he was haunted by that thought: if they were to burst in right now, the Cossacks, the Nazis, the BNP, any gang of thugs: he would be the man who blubbers and shits himself. And he was ashamed.

———

The following morning Rabbi Feldman ventured out into a world that seemed irredeemably changed: where once he felt pride at his place in his community, now he felt only numbness, like he wasn't really there. Everywhere he went he was greeted with enthusiasm, hearty congratulations, even admiration, but each word of praise just added to the weight of shame within his heart. He couldn't even look at his synagogue, the thought of it filled him with a panic. It stood there, a big black shadow, looming, unavoidable, in front of his house. But business is business, and he had already taken ten days off. As Mrs Feldman had said, he had to get back on the saddle and pedal with all his might – before he knew it he would be back at the top of the hill. She did like colourfully extended metaphors. And in any case, to that end she had arranged a meeting with the synagogue council and public relations committee for three o'clock.

As with all such meetings it was generally tedious, and he left all the note-taking to his wife, who was also the Honourable Secretary, contenting himself with nodding periodically. The final item on the agenda was the burglary. First the rabbi was formally congratulated and applauded for his quick thinking and bravery. Estimates for the insurance claim were reported, amounting to less than four thousand pounds, which was better than anyone had initially expected. Then came the issue of the press coverage. The PR manager spoke with a barely disguised tone of restrained excitement.

'As you are all aware, this incident has generated an unprecedented amount of coverage, and frankly ...' he paused for dramatic effect before concluding 'it's all good! As they like to say nowadays, the thing's gone viral. I mean, hell, I've even found us mentioned in the *Kiwi Herald* ... Now the big question is, what do we want to do with it? We need to strike whilst the iron's hot or in a week or two it will be yesterday's news. So ...? What do we think?'

'Surely the first question is do we want to do anything with it?' asked Mrs Feldman. 'I mean, just because it made the papers. To my mind, and I am sure I also speak for the rabbi here, wouldn't it be better to just carry on as if nothing had happened? The insurance is covering all the damage, and, so far as I can see, it's all over. What more is there to do?'

'With all due respect to the Honourable Secretary here, I couldn't disagree more. This is a once in a lifetime opportunity. If we play it right we could become the most famous synagogue in Britain.'

'And what would that serve?'

'Well, for a start it could bring in international funding.'

'But for what? To what end?' Mrs Feldman was becoming irritated. This wasn't the first time she and Mr Hanflig had clashed over issues of policy. 'Might I remind our young Public Relations Officer that our single duty here is to serve the community, not line our own pockets, nor plan future career moves.'

At this Mr Roschwald, the Honourable Chairman, stepped in.

'Please, Mrs Feldman. Let's not make this personal. We understand that you want to protect the rabbi. It seems to me that before we can usefully discuss this further we need to clarify a few things. Let's be honest. The press weren't interested in our wonderful synagogue, nor Judaism, nor our community or what we do, etcetera, etcetera. No, there were two things which caught their imagination: firstly the bravery of Rabbi Feldman, who put both his life and his dignity on the line to save our synagogue. That much isn't in question. And might I again commend both his courage and devotion to this building and everything it stands for.'

A general chorus of approval from all assembled quickly developed into a brief burst of applause, causing the rabbi to blush and shift on his chair uncomfortably.

'The second point is this whole business of the alleged miracle. Now we all know that this has been somewhat exaggerated by the coverage. But nonetheless shots were fired, the rabbi was unharmed, and our beautiful synagogue was saved, and that is in itself something of a miracle. But that's not the miracle they are writing about. No, they are making something of a fuss out of the rabbi's tallis; and this is the part that should concern us: Rabbi Feldman here has assured us that his tallis remains unmarked by the incident, yet the papers are claiming it is riddled with bullet holes. Of course, whether wearing the tallis, exclusively as it were, encouraged the Lord's protection is not for us to say. But that is the story. The question is, is this a story we can endorse?'

'Really Mr Chairman, from a PR perspective, the actuality of the bullet holes themselves is not important. It's the miracle that will sell it.'

'Sell what?' snapped Mrs Feldman. 'What is it you're so keen to sell? We're not a business. We have no products.'

'That is where the Honourable Secretary is mistaken. We do have a product. A very saleable product, at this moment. We have the Miraculous Rabbi Feldman.' He said this last phrase as if unveiling a statue.

'I must object!' Mrs Feldman almost fell off her chair.

'Please, Mrs Feldman, let Mr Hanflig put his case. You will have your chance shortly.'

'Thank you, Mr Chairman. As I was saying, we have the Miraculous Rabbi Feldman. Think about it; it's perfect. It encompasses all the elements that got them excited, in one bold package. First we need to get the rabbi on TV and radio, whilst the iron's still hot, to cement his product image; then I see regular slots on *Question Time, Thought for the Day*, any public debates involving religion or ethics, anything of that kind. If we play it right this could be the brand that marks our humble synagogue out from all the others. And what with the potential worldwide interest, it could, just could, go global.'

'And how exactly would that benefit the synagogue?' The Chairman was sceptical, but curious nonetheless.

'Prestige, Mr Chairman. Prestige and authority. The very currencies of the religious market we are all competing in. Think about it. What does a miracle actually mean? It means we have the backing of God himself, not to mention the tabloid press. And both of those are more than bankable. All we need to do is play the game, through our figurehead, our brand, so to speak, the Miraculous Rabbi Feldman, and then we're away.'

The Chairman looked across the table at the rabbi, who had grown increasingly pale throughout the discussion, but then turned to Mrs Feldman, as experience had taught him to always address her first, where the rabbi was concerned, and otherwise.

'Mrs Feldman, I believe you might have some comments.'

Mrs Feldman, who had been literally on the edge of her seat with agitation, immediately launched into a great tirade against Mr Hanflig, his entire profession and the commercialisation of religion as a whole. Even she was surprised by her vehemence. Finally, as if playing a trump card, she gestured dramatically towards her husband.

'I mean, just look at the poor rabbi, hasn't he been through enough already?'

There was a brief silence as they all looked at Rabbi Feldman, who immediately turned even paler and began to shake.

'I cannot believe the lack of ambition in this room!'

'Mr Hanflig, please.' The Chairman returned his attention to Rabbi Feldman. 'rabbi, this involves you more than anyone else. What do you think?'

Rabbi Feldman thought everyone was looking at him, expecting a response. They wanted to make him some kind of hero, but he knew that if the enemy were to burst in now, he would be the man that blubbered and shat himself. The shame rose up through him, causing his shaking to become more violent. He tried to speak, but all that came out was a broken stammer.

'I, I, i ii I … i i i …'

It was more than he could bear, and before he realised what was happening he had run from the room, down the stairs and into the main Sanctuary, the place where it had all happened, the place he had not dared to enter since that fateful Sunday night. He strode purposefully towards the Ark, driven as much by anger as by shame, then flung himself face down on the carpet before it and began to pray, a pleading, desperate prayer that only those who have seen some truth and need to forget, would recognise.

He didn't know how long he lay there, but when he finally pushed himself back up into the world Mrs Feldman was standing over him, her kindly eyes offering a brief refuge from all the torment and despair eating at his soul.

—

That night Rabbi Feldman had the most vivid dream of his life. He was wandering alone in a vast desert. It was night, a cold, pitch-black night with no moon, no stars, yet even so he could somehow see his way. He knew that he must keep going, he must get to the other side, but was confused by his compass, which made no sense to him, and soon he was entirely lost. Just as he was giving up hope a snake slithered across his path and so he followed it deeper into the barren rocky landscape. Eventually they came to a solitary bush. The snake coiled itself tightly around the stem, and it burst into white flames.

And then the flames spoke to the rabbi.

'Walter,' said the flames, 'I am the God of your Fathers, the God of Isaac and Abraham, of all the Jewish people.'

Rabbi Feldman immediately prostrated himself on the rocky ground before the bush, then remembering the strictures against exactly that in the Torah, sat upright; though he was Reform, in the presence of the Lord G-d himself he felt it only respectful to behave as if Orthodox.

'I will answer your question,' the bush continued, its voice a hiss and crackle. 'You cried out to know why I would step in to save your life, only to leave you humiliated; though really that is two questions. Firstly, why did I save you – initially curiosity, it's not often I hear Kaddish recited by a rabbi wearing only his tallis, and in preparation for your own imminent death, too; quite a scene, quite poetic in its way, for that alone you deserved a break. As for the humiliation, that wasn't my work, you did that all by yourself.'

But just as those last words were shrinking back into the flames the earth began to violently shake, and a tremendous thundering rent the sky, leaving a jagged white crack across the whole of the heavens. And from this crack erupted a voice, fiery as lava, smooth as honey, deep as darkest space itself.

'Enough!' it roared, and the fiery bush was extinguished, leaving only a scorched stump.

'Walter,' continued the great voice more gently, 'you are a fool!'

Again the ground shook, this time causing the rabbi to support himself on all fours in a desperate bid not to fall on his face, which failed. Then suddenly, a deep rumbling beneath him ripped its way through the ground where the bush had stood, and a magnificent spiral staircase rose up towards the heavens, sprouting branches as it grew, and where the tips touched the sky, he could see angels, glittering as they drifted up and down on invisible currents, like golden leaves gusting in a celestial breeze. Walking down the main trunk of the staircase, or rather gliding a foot or so above the steps, was a bearded man, aged around thirty, with long straggly blond hair, and wearing a simple sackcloth robe.

'Yes, I know what you're thinking,' said the bearded man as he reached the bottom of the staircase, 'that I look like Jesus, but really I can assure you, beard and sandals was a good look for many thousands of years, and will be again, and in any case, I was dressing like this long before he was even thought of. But listen, we need to have a chat, you and I, so I thought it best to appear in a more human form. Had you been Orthodox I would have stuck with the boom and bluster, but since you are Reform …'

The man, who was much taller than Rabbi Feldman, took him by the shoulder and led him away from the staircase into the blackness of the midnight desert. With a gesture of his hand he healed the crack across the heavens and everything was dark again.

'As I was saying, you are a fool, Walter. But a well-meaning fool, and is it not said that if a fool were to persist in his folly he would become wise? But now three times you have let ha-satan trick you. And, you know, three strikes and you're out! Hah! Only joking. But that last time, I mean he appeared to you as a snake, but still you took him at his word; claiming to be me, the cheek of it! Now I'm not one to condemn a little healthy mischief, but really, something has to be done. He is getting a little too cocky, seeing what goes on down here, and this is the thing, none of it is about you. What he wants is a symbol, and symbols, they are dangerous things, particularly when in the wrong hands, you understand, like the apple, or the golden calf, the Turin shroud, that was also one of his, or the Pope. And that, Walter, is what he wants to make of your tallis. Normally, of course I wouldn't interfere, really I'm not interfering now, I just want to help you along your way a little. After all, it's no more your fault that you are a fool than it is mine that I am great.'

They had reached an oasis, the black water reflecting the black silhouettes of black palm trees against a dark black sky.

'So, Walter, you see many people are going to want that tallis; even now ha-satan is fuelling their desire, but you must only give it to the one whose intentions are sincere.'

'But how will I know?'

'Oh, you will know. It will be imperative. All you have to do is hold on to the tallis until then. I have faith in you, Walter.'

At that the bearded man smiled, and Rabbi Feldman felt a profound warmth rise up from his belly, like a large gulp of fine scotch whisky.

'And Walter, you will deny me three times before the Sabbath falls … but worry not, it's the fourth that hits the mark.'

'Now,' he gestured with his hand in a great arc, lighting the moon and stars in its wake, 'now, Walter, I think you must wake up and smell the coffee. You have a busy day ahead of you.'

Suddenly Rabbi Feldman found he was awake, back in his bedroom, and sure enough, Mrs Feldman was just coming through the door, carrying a tray with a cup of coffee, and his favourite breakfast pastry.

———

He didn't mention his dream to anyone, as it was only a dream, and, in truth, he was both perplexed and a little embarrassed by its Christian overtones. But it had lightened his mood a little, and if he were really honest, there was a small part of him that quietly believed it was a real vision, despite the larger part telling him not to be so ridiculous. Either way, vision or dream, it had given him a glimpse of hope that his current torment might have an ending, a feeling that lasted throughout breakfast and his morning ablutions, right up until he left the house and crossed the street towards his synagogue, when his heart became doom-laden once again.

Everyone was very kind, bringing him tea and biscuits, not asking him to make any difficult decisions, tip-toeing around him, but the kinder they were, the worse he felt. Even Mr Hanflig popped his head in to enquire after the rabbi's health and peace of mind, and only once mentioned setting up a meeting to further discuss his grand plan. For lunch the rabbi returned home where Mrs Feldman had cooked up her best chicken soup with peppered kneidlach, and a side plate of fried cheese blintzes, but even that only raised a token smile.

That afternoon he had one fixed appointment, with Simon Kohn of the Chabad, at four-thirty, so decided to take a nap. Really he was hoping for another vision, but if he did dream at all, it left no impression.

Simon Kohn, a tall and surprisingly handsome young man, despite the uneven side-locks and rather patchy beard, arrived promptly at four-thirty, bearing gifts: a bottle of slivovitz and a jar of homemade pickled herrings from his wife. Rabbi Feldman had always been a little suspicious of the Lubavitchers, as he was of anyone who took religious books too literally, but this Simon Kohn seemed an amenable young man. However, after five minutes or so of the necessary pleasantries, the rabbi decided to push the conversation to its point.

'So, Mr Kohn, what brings you here? I assume you haven't come all this way just to ask when I last laid tefillin.'

Simon Kohn's face shaped a wry unamused smile.

'Rabbi, am I so transparent? But you are of course right. And I am sure you know it is the small matter of the *miracle*.' He said that last word as if it were foreign to his mouth, but also sweet and a little chewy.

'Of course, the miracle.' Rabbi Feldman visibly shrunk in size. 'Everyone wants to know about the miracle. But really, there was no miracle. It's all rumours and exaggeration, tittle-tattle, but still they printed it in the newspapers, you know how they are.'

Simon Kohn was not a man to be fazed at first refusal. 'Before you answer, rabbi, perhaps you should first hear the question ...'

He gave the rabbi a look which demanded he pay proper attention.

'I know you think all of us at Chabad are, shall we say, deluded, it's okay, and we think you are perhaps a little lax in your interpretations ... You agree?'

'I suppose so.' Answered the rabbi, who wasn't much in the habit of agreeing with Lubavitchers, even about their disagreements.

'You see, I *know* it was G-d's hand that parted the Red Sea, but you, you probably think it was an earthquake, or drought or somesuch. Yes?'

'I believe the Red Sea parted,' the rabbi answered hesitantly.

'Parted, sure, but do you believe it was G-d's hand?'

The rabbi shrugged. 'Who can say? It was G-d's will ...'

Simon Kohn stood up and leant across the Rabbi Feldman's desk, closely fixing his eyes on the rabbi's, as if to leave no doubt as to the seriousness of his question.

'But was it G-d's hand?' He said this slowly, quietly, and with great earnestness.

The two of them remained locked eye to eye for what seemed to the rabbi far too long for polite discussion, but he wasn't going to back down so easily. He answered in the same slow, quiet tone as the question.

'I'm sure it was God's will, whether by his hand or not.'

'Exactly!' Simon Kohn sat back in his chair and smiled as if victory were already his.

'You see, I may believe one thing, and you another, but we are both good Jews, in our own way. It's the stories themselves that bind us together, literal or symbolic, historic or mythic, it matters not. As Jews we both believe and we don't believe. But we are all Jews.'

The rabbi's face screwed up a little as he began to see where this was going.

'And so, you see, in this context, your little miracle, whatever you like to call it, really it cannot be ignored. It is a gift, woven from the sinews of Judaism itself.'

'Mr Kohn, that's all very fine and grand, but there was no miracle. I was lucky. He shot. He missed.'

'But rabbi, are things ever really that simple? When the Red Sea parted to let our forefathers out of Egypt, was this a miracle? Really, it matters not. Either way we passed out of slavery, and thousands of years later we are still here, despite everything. That is the miracle.'

The rabbi's eyes betrayed his irritation, though his voice remained calm and measured.

'You are good with the words and the metaphors, Mr Kohn, I'll give you that. But what I really want is to get this whole thing behind me. Tell me, have you ever had a gun pointed at you?'

Simon Kohn was momentarily stumped. This was not a question he had prepared for, though it took but a moment for his wily smile to return.

'Me, personally, no. But if you consider Our People's history, the threat of fatal and bloody violence is omnipresent. You know that. So me, I am one of a small minority. You, on the other hand, you can stand proudly with Our Ancestors, shoulder to shoulder.'

At this Rabbi Feldman stiffened, then rose up in his chair, leant across his desk and fixed his eyes on Simon Kohn with a look that left no doubt.

'That is not how it was, Mr Kohn. I was a coward. I begged for my life. I despaired. And now I would like to move on.'

'Exactly!'

This was certainly not the response Rabbi Feldman expected, and nearly caused him to lose his determined expression.

'That is why I am here,' continued Simon Kohn. 'To make you an offer.'

'What kind of offer?'

'Let us take over this *miracle* for you.' Simon Kohn's face opened out into the smile of a man who knew he had just said something unexpected and dramatic.

'I'm not sure I understand.'

'Just that. Manage it for you. Let's be frank shall we: yours is a nice little Reform community. You're not interested in persuasion, in representing the Jewish people, inspiring, bringing our lost brothers and sisters back into the fold. None of this is your concern, nor should it be. But for us at Chabad, it is the way. It's what we do. And this miracle of yours could prove a most valuable tool.'

'I'm sorry, Mr Kohn, but what you are saying is ridiculous. How could you possibly *take it over?*'

'The tallis, rabbi, the tallis. It is the symbol that represents the miracle. Pass it on to us, and you can be done with it for good.'

Despite the confidence of his words it was clear from his tone that Simon Kohn knew he was losing, and Rabbi Feldman, picking up on this, suddenly felt he had displayed ample patience, but enough was enough. He rose up in his chair, fixed his face with the most decisive look he could muster, and was about to politely draw the conversation to a close when the ever-anticipatory Simon Kohn stood up himself.

'But rabbi, I can see you aren't ready to make a decision today. Such things need to be thought about, of course.'

He reached across the desk to shake the rabbi's hand.

'But let me leave you my card, and once you have considered you can call me, any time. And maybe, if I do not hear from you, for I know you are a busy man, maybe I'll call back here, next week perhaps.'

And with that he ushered himself out of Rabbi Feldman's office, leaving only his business card on the desk and, slight feeling of nausea in the rabbi's belly.

———

Once he had wrapped up the remaining paperwork, which was very little as everyone at the synagogue was covering for the rabbi however they could, he put on his coat and headed across the road, looking forward to watching the last hour of children's TV with Izzy, but as he turned to walk down his path he saw two people, a man and a woman whom he didn't know, waiting at his front door. They looked in their mid-twenties, properly dressed, though casual, with a look of naïve over-enthusiasm on their faces as they saw him.

'Rabbi Feldman?' said the young woman. Her voice was gentle and hesitant.

The rabbi was in no mood for strangers.

'Yes. What do you want?' He tried to make this sound polite but his heart wasn't in it.

'We'd like to talk to you, if you don't mind, and you have the time ...'

'Yes, if you have a minute. We've been waiting all afternoon.' This was the young man, whose voice was also gentle and hesitant.

Of course! Mrs Feldman had taken the children to Samuel's birthday party. He had forgotten. 'Damn it!' he thought. There was nobody here to rescue him.

'I'm sorry. I don't have the time. You'll have to call again later, maybe next week. And make an appointment with the synagogue. This is my *private* home.'

When he started speaking he had intended to end by entering his house and closing the door behind him, but the two strangers were blocking his way, forcing him to squeeze awkwardly between them, and then his key become stuck in the lock, by which time he had run out of words.

'Honestly, rabbi, this will only take a few minutes.'

'And we have been waiting for some time.'

'It's about the miracle.'

At this the rabbi stopped pulling at his key and turned to face the couple.

'I don't know who you are, but I can tell you now, there was NO

MIRACLE! So, if that is all …' and he returned to pulling at the key.

'We represent the Jews for Jesus,' said the young woman, as if it explained something relevant.

'We're here to offer our help,' added the young man.

'Our assistance,' suggested the young woman.

'And our expertise,' concluded the young man.

'But as there was no miracle your services are not required, thanks all the same.' Suddenly the key came free from the lock, causing the rabbi to stumble backwards, nearly tumbling over into the couple.

'Could we at least see the tallis?' asked the young woman as she helped him regain his balance.

'Yes, Rachel has a gift, she can *tell* things. If you would let her hold it …'

'I'd love to touch it, if that's okay …'

'I really can't help you.' He pushed the key slowly back into the lock and this time it turned. There was a click.

'Well, okay … but if you change your mind, please do call us.' The young man offered the rabbi a business card which he reluctantly accepted, knowing escape was now imminent.

'And we'll make an appointment next week then, at the synagogue,' added the young woman.

'As you like,' replied the rabbi, turning the second key in the second lock. Finally the door opened.

'Do you mind if we say a prayer for you?' asked the man.

'As you like,' said the rabbi as he closed the door behind him.

The couple remained on the rabbi's doorstep, bowed their heads, and spoke a long prayer as one, commending the rabbi to God, and asking that he be shown the Light. Then they sang a hymn, in close harmony, *Climbing the Mountain*, before eventually wandering off.

All the while the rabbi was sitting on the stairs, listening, feeling trapped.

—

Half an hour later found Rabbi Feldman installed on the sofa with a large glass of whisky and ice. The TV was quietly murmuring nonsense to itself with the last hour of children's programming, but the rabbi was paying it little attention. He was thinking about the dream.

Twice today he had been asked for the tallis, just as the dream had said, and that had to be more than a coincidence. Or was it? Was he just being an old fool? He needed to talk to Mrs Feldman. She would know what was what. She should be home with the children around eight.

And so he went to the kitchen to get a couple of chocolate éclairs.

Just as he was about to return to the sofa with his prize there was a tap at the kitchen window. He turned around to see a tall man, in a black overcoat and broad-brimmed hat, though not of the standard Orthodox style, staring at him through the window, and with an uncomfortably stern expression on his face. The rabbi was in two minds. On the one hand, there was a strange man in his garden who clearly wanted his attention, on the other, he had had enough of strange men, and women, for one day, and was about to eat his éclairs. The man tapped the window again, using the nail of his forefinger. Rabbi Feldman sighed, reluctantly put the plate down on the worktop and unlocked the back door. He was just about to chastise the man for disturbing him in his private home, and trespassing in his garden at that, when the man put his finger to his lips in a manner so commanding that Rabbi Feldman found himself momentarily struck dumb. Once he was sure he had his audience the man spoke.

'Rabbi, I will come straight to the point as I know you are a busy man. My employer has an interest, a hobby shall we call it, which may be about to make you very wealthy ... Fairly wealthy.'

'Who are you?' The rabbi was interested, though he was also still rather affronted by the interruption.

'Who I am is irrelevant,' continued the stranger. 'And who my employer is, on the other hand, will remain undisclosed. All that should concern you is what we want. And ...' He gestured to a black briefcase set on the ground next to him, 'what we are offering you in return.'

Rabbi Feldman was about to say 'you want the tallis', in an exasperated though politely enquiring tone, but before he had even taken a breath the stranger once again put his finger to his lips.

'My employer is willing ... happy, to offer you ...' he held out the briefcase, 'twenty thousand pounds, in used bank notes, to do with as you wish; keep it for yourself, donate it to the synagogue, give it to your favourite charity, that's up to you, not our concern, and all he is asking …'

'The tallis,' interrupted the rabbi. 'You want the tallis.'

'Er, yes indeed', replied the stranger, clearly taken aback at his thunder being stolen. 'For which he is delighted to offer you the sum of twenty thousand pounds.'

'Yes, you said, but why?'

'What do you mean?'

'Why is your employer so delighted to offer me twenty thousand pounds for it?'

'I think perhaps for twenty thousand pounds you might not ask so many questions …'

'Sir, I don't know who you are but I am a rabbi, and a busy rabbi at that, not some back street gangster who does shady deals in suburban gardens when all decent people want is to be sitting down in front of the TV with a cream cake. Now please either answer my question or leave me in peace.'

'I do apologise, rabbi, I certainly didn't mean to upset you. Not at all. The truth is I have never been asked that before. Usually the money is enough. But I can see you are a man of integrity, as befits one so favoured by the Lord …'

'Please …'

'My employer is a collector of religious artefacts, and he read about …'

'If you've come about the miracle let me stop you right there.' The rabbi was rapidly losing patience, twenty thousand pounds or not; and there was something he neither liked nor trusted about this man. 'Honestly, you're wasting your time. There was no miracle, no bullet holes, no heavenly interventions. Now, if you please, I have an important appointment.' And with that the rabbi closed the door and returned his attention to his éclairs. But just as he was about to leave the kitchen with his prize he was distracted for the second time by an unfamiliar rustling sound. He turned around to see an arm reaching up through the cat flap, waving a small white card.

'Please rabbi, take your time,' said a muffled voice from the other side of the door. 'Think about it … I'll come back next week perhaps … and if you change your mind in the meantime please do give me a call …'

—

Mrs Feldman arrived home three éclairs later to find her husband sat on the sofa amidst a liberal scattering of multi-coloured sweet wrappers, muttering to himself about 'the cheek of it' and 'what am I, a crazy-magnet?' Of course, he had been right: after bathing and bedding the children, calming her husband, cooking him a light dinner and listening a number of times to his muddled explanation of the day, Mrs Feldman did indeed know what was what.

'It seems to me,' she said once the rabbi had concluded his fourth and clearest retelling, 'that this may well all be, as you put it, just so much nonsense, but as you also often say, non-sense is the most dangerous kind of sense, for it has no handle. Am I right?'

The rabbi nodded in recognition of his own wise words.

'I'm sure it will all fizzle out of its own accord given time,' continued Mrs Feldman, 'but if you really want this to be done and dusted sooner rather than later we must 'pour the tea', so to speak …' This comment related to a 'storm in a tea pot' image she had used a number of metaphors earlier, and she couldn't resist a fleeting look of glee at having managed a neat return. However, practiced as he was with his wife's colourful approach to language, the rabbi didn't adequately disguise his confusion.

'You know, bring things to a head, pour the tea …'

The rabbi still looked puzzled.

'What I mean is …' continued Mrs Feldman with the slow exasperated tone of a schoolmistress explaining something for the tenth time to a sweet but particularly dim child, 'rather than sitting around, fretting and waiting for the *crazies* to come to you one at a time, and there is nothing more persistent in this world than *crazies* of the religious variety as well you know, we should bring them all here, on our own terms … arrange a meeting, to discuss the matter.'

The rabbi was horrified by the thought of this, but he knew from experience that Mrs Feldman was invariably right about people and how they should be dealt with, so did his best to conceal the instinctive panic. Even so, his right eyebrow began to twitch a little.

'All of them?' he asked slowly. 'And that would be good because …?'

'Because that way we can sit back and let them argue it out between themselves. Give them enough rope … Then all we have to deal with is the last man swinging.' She could see her husband's increasing nervousness and added more gently, 'after all, dear, it's not you that they are after. It's the tallis.'

'That damned tallis!' muttered the rabbi. 'What was I thinking?! I'm a reform rabbi! I don't even need a tallis!'

'Yes, dear, but you like the theatre of it, as well you know,' She reached across the sofa and gently stroked his arm.

'We'll ask Mr Hanflig along too. That should help bring the kettle to a boil.' This last comment was really self-satire, contrived to make the rabbi smile, and it worked.

———

The meeting was set for eight o'clock the following Sunday evening, so as not to clash with any of the synagogue's regular activities. In the meantime, when he wasn't fulfilling his rabbinical duties, which were few as everyone was still covering for him wherever they could, Rabbi Feldman slept as much as possible, hoping for another vision, or dream, or anything more reassuring than being awake, but all he found was sleep, which was at least something.

Mr Hanflig was the first to arrive, almost an hour early, under the pretence of having to deal with a mountain of paperwork, though he was only in his office for ten minutes before taking his place in the Meeting Room. He tried to engage the rabbi and his wife in various leading conversations but they were giving nothing away, and quickly disappeared into their own offices, leaving him alone at the grand oak table, setting out his various charts.

When Rabbi Feldman returned to the Meeting Room, just as the synagogue clock was chiming eight, he found everyone waiting for him. Mrs Feldman had acted as receptionist, meeting, greeting, and locking up once everyone had arrived so that they wouldn't be disturbed, and was, at that moment, serving tea from a large metal thermos. The rabbi took his place at the head of the table, and Mrs Feldman sat next to him, offering him a sly, reassuring smile in the process. The rabbi still didn't understand what she thought would be gained by this meeting, but she clearly had a plan, and seemed to be enjoying herself. He looked around the table, trying to disguise his nervousness. They were all here: Simon Kohn, the Lubavitcher; the two Jews for Jesus whose names he couldn't remember; the man with the briefcase, still wearing his coat and hat, and of course Mr Hanflig, whose charts took up half the table. But despite Mrs Feldman's many insistences over the last few days that he was in control of this meeting, and that he wouldn't have to say a word if he didn't want to, the rabbi couldn't help feeling more like he was on trial, facing a host of accusers.

'So,' began Mrs Feldman, 'shall we call this meeting to order?'

There was a general murmur of affirmation.

'Well, as you all know,' she continued, 'we have gathered here today to discuss what, if anything,' she looked briefly at her husband, 'should be done to best take advantage of the publicity that blew up following the attempted burglary.'

'Not really,' interrupted Simon Kohn, 'if I might interrupt. The publicity is secondary. It is the tallis that is of concern.'

'And the miracle,' added the woman from Jews for Jesus.

'The tallis *is* the miracle,' retorted Simon Kohn with a somewhat patronising tone. 'Whatever else may or may not have occurred, the Lord in his wisdom has turned this tallis into a symbol, and as such it is our duty to make use of it. And by us I mean Jews.' He looked accusingly at the woman.

'We are Jews!' demanded the man from Jews for Jesus. 'We have just accepted that Jesus is the Messiah. Why should that make us less Jewish than you? Jesus was a Jew after all!'

'Please, let's be clear, this has nothing to do with God!' Mr Hanflig butted in. 'And everything to do with PR.'

'Everything has something to do with G-d, Mr Hanflig! As every good Jew should know!' Simon Kohn stated pointedly, looking first at Mr Hanflig and then casting an accusatory glance at the Jews for Jesus.

'My employer is prepared to double his previous offer,' added the man in the broad-brimmed hat, somewhat out of context.

'Gentlemen, lady, please ...' demanded Mrs Feldman in her best schoolmistress voice, 'can we keep this to the point?' She turned to her husband. 'rabbi, have you brought the tallis in question?'

The rabbi grunted and placed a see-through plastic zip-up bag on the table which Mrs Feldman took from him, unzipped, removed the tallis, and with a single expert flick of her wrist, unfolded it neatly across the table, sending Mr Hanflig's charts drifting to the floor. There was a murmur of puzzlement around the table.

'That's not the tallis!' said the man from Jews for Jesus.

'Where are the bullet holes?' added the woman.

'As I believe the rabbi has already tried to explain to you all, there are no bullet holes.'

'But we saw the pictures, in the newspapers …'

'Do I really need to tell you not to believe everything you read in the newspapers, young lady?!' said Mrs Feldman sternly. 'And in any case, if you read the captions properly you would know they were pictures of what the tallis *might* look like.'

'That does somewhat diminish the potential PR value,' commented Mr Hanflig.

'And raise certain questions about the Lord's intentions,' added Simon Kohn.

'I need to consult with my employer,' said the man in the broad-brimmed hat. 'May I step outside to make a phone call?'

'It's all locked up. You can use my office if you need to. Through that door there.' Mrs Feldman gestured towards a black wooden door with a large glass window on the other side of the Meeting Room. The man in the broad-brimmed hat stood up, politely nodded his head at those assembled and disappeared into Mrs Feldman's office, taking his briefcase with him.

'But even so, a miracle's a miracle,' said the woman from Jews for Jesus once the office door was closed.

'That's certainly true, and the Lord does work in mysterious ways,' added the man.

'Yes, but without the bullet holes it has no symbolic power,' said Simon Kohn, again in a distinctly patronising tone.

'Maybe the bullets bounced off,' suggested the woman, ignoring Simon Kohn.

'That would be an even better miracle!' said the man, enthusiastically.

At that moment the air was riven with an explosive bang sending a spray of splinters into the air, most of which landed on Mr Hanflig.

'Maybe the bullets bounced off! You fuckers! What the fuck are you fuckers talking about!' It was a young thug's voice, sarcastic, threatening, distinctly working class, and it was coming from above them. They all looked up to see a gun pointed at them from the gallery, in the hands of a tall young man with a skinhead haircut, who fitted the description of the armed burglar who had got away. It was Jonny.

'Well I think I've fucking answered that one, haven't I?' He let off two more shots into the tallis. The Jews for Jesus both screamed and clutched each other's hands whilst Mr Hanflig hid under the table, whimpering for his mother with tears running down his cheeks.

Jonny slowly made his way down the steps from the gallery, keeping the gun pointed at the Feldmans.

'I wasn't expecting Fatty here to be having friends over. But the rest of you listen up. My business is with him. You lot behave yourselves and you'll come out of this unhurt. You get me?'

The Jews for Jesus nodded and clutched each other's hands even tighter and Simon Kohn slid under the table to join Mr Hanflig, who promptly shat himself, then continued whimpering. Out of sight Mrs Feldman grabbed her husband's knee.

Jonny was now down the stairs and heading towards them.

'So, Fatty Feldman, That is your name isn't it? You see, you and I have got some business that needs finishing. Because *you* have made *me* a laughing stock!'

He stopped, about two metres away, keeping the gun on Rabbi Feldman.

'They're calling me a fucking joke! Saying that I was scared off by a naked fat old man! And you had to go and talk to the newspapers, didn't you? So now everybody knows about it. You see, I can't have that. I can't have everybody thinking I'm a fucking joke, 'cause that's not good for business. So I've got to send out a message. You get me? So people know not to call Jonny a joke.'

He took a step forward towards the rabbi and suddenly shouted in his face.

'BECAUSE JONNY IS NO FUCKING JOKE!'

Still the rabbi and Mrs Feldman remained sat as they were, frozen, their eyes fixed on the intruder. But it was too much for the Jews for Jesus who both began to cry.

'Will you two shut up and get under the table.' Jonny waved the gun in their general direction and they immediately disappeared under the table. Then he returned his attention to the rabbi.

'So, we're going to continue where we left off, only this time I've got a gun that FUCKING WORKS!'

He let off a shot into the ceiling to demonstrate, and a series of stifled shrieks spluttered from under the table. Simon Kohn shat himself.

'So, this is how it's gonna be. It's too late for you, I'm sure you can understand that, but if you play along nicely then nobody else will get hurt. You get me?'

The white-faced rabbi nodded, but Mrs Feldman had had enough.

'No, we don't get that. Who the hell do you think you are, coming in here waving your pathetic little gun around like some Nazi thug who's watched too many gangster films.' And with that she stood up defiantly, but Jonny immediately landed a powerful punch on her nose, sending her flying backwards into the wall where she slumped to the ground, semi-conscious.

Seeing his wife attacked so brutally sent the rabbi's head spinning. It was as if he relived everything that had happened since the burglary in a single instant: the humiliation, the despair, the smell of shit in his mouth and nostrils, the realisation that he was a coward, the dream, and all the visitors, every one of them wanting a piece of him. And suddenly that thing inside him snapped for the second and last time in his long life.

'I will not be that man!' He screamed as he jumped up, grabbed the large stainless steel thermos of tea and swung it at Jonny, catching him hard on the shoulder and knocking the gun from his hand.

'I am not a coward!' he shouted as he swung a second time, hitting Jonny on the side the head, sending him staggering backwards.

'And nobody hits my Gretel!' He swung the thermos again but this time Jonny caught it, and shoved it back at the rabbi, hitting him square in the face, and he collapsed onto the floor in a daze. When his vision cleared a few seconds later he saw Jonny standing over him with the gun.

'Now you've really fucking pissed me off.' He pointed the gun at the rabbi's head. But Rabbi Feldman just smiled back at him, blood trickling from his mouth. He had proven he was not the kind of man who blubbers and shits himself and no longer cared what Jonny did to him.

'Time for Jonny bye-byes.'

Jonny pulled the trigger; Mrs Feldman shrieked; but there was no bang.

'What the fuck! I don't fucking believe it.' He pulled out the clip, checked it for bullets, replaced it, pointed the gun back at the rabbi's head and pulled the trigger a second time. Still no bang; just a quiet metal click.

'This is fucking ridiculous!'

He pointed the gun at the celling, pulled the trigger, and this time a shot did ring out, hitting a marble cornice then ricocheting back across the room where it caught Jonny across the forehead, and he fell to the floor, unmoving, blood pooling around his face.

Then there was silence.

The next thing any of them knew, the man in the broad-brimmed hat was back in the room. He headed straight for Jonny, kicked the gun into a corner, then knelt down and examined the head wound, finally checking the neck for a pulse.

'The little bastard's still alive but he'll be out for a good long while. The bullet's embedded in his thick skull, didn't quite reach the brain ... shame. You'd better call an ambulance, oh, and the police, of course.'

Having satisfied himself that Jonny was no longer a threat he walked over to the table and poked his head underneath to see Mr Hanflig, Simon Kohn and the two Jews for Jesus all huddled together quietly whimpering to themselves, smelling like a sewer.

'You guys can come out now,' though none of them moved an inch.

Suddenly Mrs Feldman awoke from her shocked daze and rushed across the room to her husband, who was still sat on the floor, smiling almost stupidly, with blood dribbling from his mouth. The two of them embraced each other tightly, and the rabbi whispered something in his wife's ear that made her hug him even closer, and smile herself.

'Well,' said the man in the broad-brimmed hat, 'it looks like we've solved the problem with the tallis.' He held it up to show three clear bullet holes, charred around the edges, very similar to the pictures in the newspapers.

'My offer still stands, double the previous offer, forty thousand ...'

'You still want it? After all of this?' asked the rabbi.

'Absolutely. All the more so. I get paid on commission,' replied the man in the broad-brimmed hat, as he carefully folded the prayer shawl and returned it to its plastic pack.

'Take it. You want it that much, it's yours.' At that moment nothing concerned the rabbi less than the tallis.

'Excellent,' said the man in the broad-brimmed hat. 'Now if you don't mind, one thing that isn't in my job description is being questioned by the police, so I'll be saying goodbye. I'm sure we won't meet again.'

He placed the briefcase on the floor next to the rabbi, then turned to leave.

'But the police will want to talk to you ...' demanded Mrs Feldman.

'I wouldn't concern yourselves. My employer is very well connected.' And with that he was gone.

'And the synagogue's all locked up ...' added Mrs Feldman almost silently after he had left.

———

The police and ambulance arrived about ten minutes later. Johnny was rushed to the Royal Free Hospital under police guard, where he was successfully operated upon and regained consciousness a couple of days later. He was remanded in custody pending his trial but escaped on the way to the courthouse.

Mr Hanflig, Simon Kohn and the Jews for Jesus, who were still under the table when the medics arrived, were treated for shock. When questioned the next day by the police they gave dramatically differing accounts of the evening, though they all agreed that Rabbi Feldman had heroically saved the day, and, most likely, their lives.

Both the Feldmans suffered a pair of black eyes, much to Izzy's amusement, as pandas were his favourite animal, and the rabbi had also lost a tooth and needed a couple of stitches to his forehead. But what surprised everyone, especially his wife, was the sudden and complete change in his spirits. To say he was back to his old self didn't quite cover it: he became pro-active, actually making decisions, expressing opinions, and even went on a diet, though that didn't last long. One of his first decisions was to hold a press conference, against Mr Hanflig's advice, in which he made it quite clear that this was all an act of common thuggery, so as to nip any further talk of miracles in the bud. He gave half the money from the briefcase to a charity working towards providing clean drinking water to both Jews and Palestinians living in Gaza, and with the other half booked a family cruise around the Mediterranean for the following summer. He often puzzled over the dream, and did have another similar 'vision' a few weeks later, but once awake considered elements within it too ridiculous to be taken seriously, so kept it to himself. As for the jamming of the gun: nobody ever spoke about that, though privately they each did wonder from time to time. But if there was one change in her husband that warmed Mrs Feldman's heart more than any other, it was that he started calling her *my Gretel.*

Oh, and nobody ever saw or heard of the man in the broad-brimmed hat again.

# Klezmer

*... and as he took up his violin, the plaintive strains gently wafted along the quiet streets of Golders Green, spreading upon their sobbing melodies the rich flavours of age-old Jewish tradition, filling many a heart with pride at who they were: women in A-line skirts and ill-fitting nylon wigs stopped their gossiping for a moment to listen; old men with long beards popped their heads out of windows and smiled; babies stopped crying; and all the world around said a broche ...*

''Scuse me mate, where's that song from?'

Daniel was awoken from his reverie by a petite Asian young man in bright orange sports clothes and a baseball cap. He made a point of concluding the phrase he was playing before answering.

'Sorry?'

'Where's that song from, mate?'

'It's an old Hungarian Jewish tune called "Haneros Hallelu".'

'I fought it sounded a bit Indian. Do you do any Nigel Kennedy?'

'I'm sorry, I only play Jewish music. If you're interested I have CDs for sale.' He pointed at the pile of CDs in his violin case.

'No worries, mate. Catch yer later,' and he was off.

Daniel was used to such interruptions; it was all part of the gig. He took a moment to straighten up his CDs, counted out five pounds in small change from his case and put it in his pocket ('never let them think you're doing too well'), then picked up his fiddle and began to play again. This time it was a Lithuanian Jewish tune, traditionally performed whilst leading the groom to the wedding chuppa. Further up the High Street he could see a group of Chassidim in long coats and broad-brimmed hats slowly making their way towards him, and imagined them to be the groom's procession. He carefully timed the emotional climax of the piece for the moment they passed him, but to no avail. Not one eye had turned in his direction. If he could catch an eye he knew he had a good chance of a coin drop. It was all about the eyes. You use the eyes to reel them in, catch them with the patter, and then, if you're lucky, you might even get a CD sale.

He was three tunes on before he spotted his next likely customer – an older, obviously middle-class woman, not Orthodox, she was too well dressed for that; and probably English; a definite possibility. She was slowing a little as she approached him, hopefully listening. Yes, he caught her eye, now she was coming towards him. He quickly drew the tune he was playing to a natural sounding conclusion.

'Feel free to take a look,' and he gestured towards the CDs with his bow.

'What was that you were playing?' She was very well-spoken. That also was a good sign.

'It's an old Russian Jewish tune. They used to play it during wedding feasts, to make the bride cry.'

'Why would they want to do that?'

'I think the idea is that she cries at the passing of her old childish life, before dancing in celebration at the start of her new life, as a wife and mother.'

'I see ... You play very beautifully.' She was getting out her purse.

'Thank you.'

'I'm Jewish myself. Are you?' She seemed to be opening the part of her purse for notes, not coins. Was she going to buy a CD?

'I'm half Jewish.'

'On which side?'

'My mother's,' he lied.

'Then you're Jewish!' She took a £10 note out of her purse and handed it to him.

'Thank you. Would you like a CD?'

'I don't have a player, I'm afraid. Good luck.' And she headed on her way.

Wow! A ten-pound note! That was rare. He carefully tucked it into his back pocket. Maybe Golders Green wasn't such a bad pitch after all. He had been beginning to doubt the place, but some spots are just like that: no response whatever for half an hour and then suddenly, a tenner. That was often the way with the quieter high streets; they suited his playing best, fewer potential customers but a better environment for them to appreciate his music, and that meant larger drops and more potential sales.

He mostly liked the slower tunes, relishing their emotional charge, playing the plaintive fiddler of folklore, wresting tragedy from the depths of his ancestral soul, but that unexpected ten-pound note had lightened his mood a little and he started up with *Fun der Chuppa*, one of a number of lively wedding dances he knew that went by that generic name. He wiggled a little as he played, enjoying the rhythm, until he noticed someone was watching him; another woman, of a similar age, in a bold red coat with upturned fur collar and a woollen hat. She had stopped and was staring at him from the other side of the street. 'You never know ...' he thought, 'could be my lucky day,' and he subtly moved into *Dybbuk Shers*, a slow and haunting set of Russian Jewish tunes, to reel her in. But after a minute or so she continued on her way. Still, he thought, high street shopping is a two-way affair. She may drop him some coins on her way back.

Ten minutes or so later the young Asian guy was back.

''Ere mate, you do sessions?'

Daniel was always surprised at how rude people can be, never waiting until the end of a phrase before bothering him with questions. He wilfully continued but drew his tune to a premature close.

'What?'

'Do you do sessions? Recording sessions?'

Daniel had answered this question hundreds of times.

'That depends ... what kind?'

'Me and me mate have a little studio, you know ... knock out beats. I was thinking we could get some Asian-Jewish crossover going down, know what I mean. Could be well sick!'

After a few more minutes of polite conversation Daniel gave him a business card, one of the fake cards he kept in his left jacket pocket to keep the freaks at bay.

'Give me a call and maybe when I'm next up this way ...' he lied.

If there was one thing he hated more than 'world music' it was 'ethnic' solos over dance beats: *music should be pure and of the soul, not hammered onto the cross of a computer-generated straightjacket.* He said it so often it was almost a motto. Anyone who knew him knew that.

———

The following hour or so passed uneventfully: he made around fifteen pounds, sold no CDs, and amused himself watching the folk of Golders Green going about their business. It struck him that there were three main types of people on this high street. The most obvious were the Orthodox Jews, some of whom still wore polish village costumes, big round fur hats, long black satin coats, side-locks and beards; but more often wore the same navy blue nylon suit and trilby for the men, long coats and headscarves or wigs for the women. These people it seemed were very unlikely to drop him anything. Then there were the rich foreigners with bad taste: there seemed to be people from every corner of the world here, each having acquired, alongside obvious financial success, a certain Golders Green aesthetic for gratuitous and aesthetically misjudged display. These people had possibilities; they would probably drop money but be unlikely to buy CDs. But most important were the cultured English middle classes, here with an international bent. This was his ideal demographic; they might buy CDs and would probably drop one-pound or two-pound coins: they wouldn't want to be seen as the kind of people who don't give money to a talented musician. But all in all it was the Jews who had brought him here. He had been playing Jewish violin music, klezmer, for three years now, in various parts of London and the South-East, gigging with bands, busking. Today he had come to Golders Green to play to traditional Jews, to bring them back their traditional music, music that had been lost in the great upheavals of the twentieth century, but had now been pieced together by a small but devoted band of New Klezmorim, of which he was one.

'Why are you doing this?'

He had been lost in another reverie and hadn't noticed the woman in the red coat.

'I said why are you doing this? Playing Yiddish music in the streets like a common beggar?'

'I'm just playing music, trying to earn a living.'

'Why Yiddish music?!'

'Well, I'm Jewish.'

'Then you should know better! By doing this you're dragging all of us back to the Ghetto!' She had turned and was walking off. 'Go home! Join an orchestra!'

He had, over the years, received a fair amount of abuse, it was a hazard of the trade, but this was by far the most perplexing. He was momentarily stunned into silence, then decided to do a coin count, removing another five pounds in change. Forty pounds; ten pounds more and he could call it a day, and so he struck up with a tune that he knew as *Merlin 2*, as it had been the second tune taught to someone he knew by a clarinettist called Merlin.

It was almost another hour before he hit his target, with the last sixty-five pence taking an annoying fifteen minutes. Then, just as he was kneeling down to pack up his fiddle, he noticed an older gentleman standing over him, with a short grey beard, wearing the uniform navy blue suit of an Orthodox Jew.

'My wife asked me to give you this,' and he passed Daniel a five-pound note.

'Oh, thank you. I was just packing up.'

'I wonder, would you mind playing me a couple of tunes ... so I can hear what all the fuss is about ...'

'Sure, no problem'. Five pounds was well worth another few minutes, and so he struck up with *The Rooster is Already Crowing*, a highly ornamented slow Hungarian Jewish folk song, followed by *Alter Kakers Tants*, a quirky Moldavian hora. All the while the elderly gentleman stood stock still and listened as if entranced. When Daniel had finished the man left a respectful few seconds of pause before he spoke.

'You play very well, with much heart.' He said this as if he really meant it, causing Daniel to pull a slightly embarrassed smirk.

'Thank you.'

'Come, let me buy you a coffee. You must be in need of refreshment and I would like to talk to you.'

Daniel was happy to go along; after all, you never know where such random encounters might lead. Buskers frequently told tales that started, 'This guy came up to me when I was busking ...' and ended with bizarre, surreal situations, extraordinary gigs, the gift of a better instrument, or the discovery of a wondrous stash of forgotten repertoire. And anyway, he had promised himself to try to follow opportunities through more often, he had let too many slip by in the past.

The cafe was surprisingly quiet for a Thursday lunchtime.

'So, my name is Josef, Josef Mautner,' the old man opened, once they had sat down with their drinks.

'Daniel Trevis.'

'Well, Daniel, you play very nicely. And you are Jewish?'

'Yes, well, half-Jewish ... on my father's side.'

Josef smiled at this. 'Then to my wife you would not be Jewish at all ... But the great David Ben-Gurion, first prime minister of Israel, he said that for him a Jew was anyone who was foolish enough to declare himself so ... and if that's good enough for him, it should be good enough for me, and for you ... So yes, you are Jewish. What was that first tune you played?'

'"Szol a Kakas Mar" – The Rooster is Already Crowing. It's an old Hungarian Jewish song. Well actually it's an old Hungarian folk song that was adopted by Jews as a Zionist freedom song during the nineteenth century.'

'So, you are a Zionist?'

'Well, not really, no, not at all. But I always make a point of playing a few Hungarian Jewish tunes whenever I perform, because not one Hungarian Jewish musician survived the holocaust. We only know of a handful of tunes, from the surviving gypsy musicians who used to play with klezmer bands at weddings before the war. So I make a point of playing them, to keep them alive.'

This was all well-rehearsed busking patter.

'So your family, they're Hungarian?'

'No. My father's family were from Amsterdam.'

'Really.' Josef paused a moment as if he had made a point. 'And where did you learn all this?'

'About Hungarian klezmer? From a CD by a band called Musikas: *The Lost Jewish Music of Transylvania*. It comes with an excellent booklet.'

'Well, you played it very beautifully. You have the soul. And that is not so common.'

'Thank you.'

'Don't thank me yet, Daniel. You don't know what I'm going to say.' He paused, and then let out a deep sigh before continuing.

'You see, my wife, she is a woman, she thinks with her heart. But that doesn't make her wrong. Usually she turns out to be right. I think with my head, and in the end I am often wrong. But my wife, she was very upset. She wanted me to come and talk to you. She said she was rude, and that's not like her, but then she was upset.' He paused for a moment to drink some coffee. 'I am not upset. I think I understand.'

'I'm sorry,' Daniel interrupted. 'I don't think I quite get what you mean.'

'No I don't think you do ... Let me ask you, why did you come here today, to Golders Green?'

'To play music. And to earn a few pennies through my efforts.'

'To play Yiddish music?'

'Yes.'

'To Jewish people?'

'Yes, I guess so.'

'And you learnt this Yiddish music from books and CDs, am I right?'

'Well, in part. Also from other musicians.'

'Who learnt from books and CDs?'

'I guess so.'

Josef took another sip of coffee, and Daniel followed suit.

'You see, to my wife, that music which you play, very nicely as I say, that music, it is the soundtrack to hundreds of years of misery, the accompaniment to the very darkest years of European Jewish history. It is the music of the shtetls, the pogroms, of hunger and fear and never knowing what was coming next. Her parents were born in a shtetl, just north of Lodz, they spent half of their lives trying to escape that world, and the next half trying to become British, to fit here. So you see, to my wife, the Old World, it is not a cause for nostalgia, it is a thing of horror. And to see you, playing that music, your case open asking for money ... well, it was as if she had stepped back in time, back to the shtetl, to the dirt, the hunger, the beggars, the stories her mother used to tell her. She was very upset.'

He paused again, and then unexpectedly smiled. Daniel didn't know what to say and so remained silent.

'Now me,' continued the old man, 'I think with my head, not my heart, and I am often wrong as I have said. But to me there is much beauty in your playing. What you are missing is tradition. Books and

CDs, they do not make a tradition; a tradition is there waiting for you when you are born, it is the thing you leave behind you when you die. And it is not yours to do with as you wish, it is an unwieldy thing, it has inertia and is a difficult thing to change, it makes it difficult for you to change ... And it is not a thing that can be acquired, at least not without great effort and commitment.'

'But I don't just learn the tunes,' Daniel insisted. 'I learn all about them, I know where each one is from, what context it was played in, in some cases what it symbolised, you know, I have done my research.'

Josef leant forward a little towards Daniel.

'Tell me, Daniel, you know a lot of tunes associated with weddings, yes?'

'Yes, most of the tunes I play.'

'And have you considered why so many tunes should be written for weddings?'

'Well, weddings were great celebrations. Some of them would last three whole days and nights, and the guests needed entertaining ...'

'Yes, yes, but why? Why would so much time and effort and expense be put aside for a wedding? ... Amongst people so poor ... Well?'

Daniel knew the question was rhetorical and so just shrugged to fill the gap.

'It's because a wedding was one brief moment when everyone could come together and pretend that love can indeed triumph over all the misery and the fear and the hunger that stalk ordinary days. That is why Yiddish music is so steeped in sadness, because there was much misery to express. But here, today, in Golders Green, there is no value in reminding us of miseries past; here, every day there is some cause for joy. We don't want to keep our heads to the ground anymore; here we want to look to the sky ... because we can. Do you see?'

'I see what you mean, but I have to say I think you're wrong.' His voice rose a pitch defensively. 'If I understand you, you feel that this music should be left to fade away, to disappear, and that I have no right to play it, to try to preserve it. But this is *my* heritage, you yourself said I have the soul for it.'

'Sure, preserve it, put in a museum, play it in concert halls, but don't try to become a *klezmer*, don't go begging with it in the streets.'

Daniel tried to disguise his irritation. This old man was getting a little under his skin.

'I'm not begging, Mr Mautner. I don't beg. I move people with my playing, and they pay me for my trouble. Today I made fifty-five pounds. So plenty of folks out there seem to appreciate it.'

'And how many of them were Jews?'

'I don't know. Some. But, that's not the point. I'm bringing the beauty of klezmer music to the public, to people that might never come across it otherwise.'

'And of course they pay you. You play very well. They are paying for your talent, they don't care what tune it is, or where it's from. They don't understand it. To them it is pretty and a little bit exotic. It has no meaning.'

Daniel made a point of looking at his watch, 'I'm sorry, Mr Mautner, I really have to go'. He stood up and began gathering his possessions.

'Daniel, I'm sorry, now I'm being rude. Please sit down a minute more.'

Daniel sat down hesitantly, keeping his hands on his bags.

'Good ... Listen, I promised my wife I would talk to you, and now I have done that. I have been the good husband; all is well with the world. Now, for you: let me do you a favour. If you are really interested in this tradition, don't read so many books. I help out a little at a small club, a Polish-Jewish club; most of our members are old, some of them were born in the Old Country, most of their parents were, and in truth, all of them are bored. Come down, talk to them, show them your enthusiasm; they may even ask you to play a tune. And you, you may learn a few things. What do you say?'

'Sure. Sounds interesting.'

Josef took a note book and pen from his coat pocket, carefully tore out a page, and wrote on it.

'Here. It's down the Hendon end of the High Street, on the left, past Klein's Bakery. We're there every evening, five 'til ten, except on the Shabbos of course.'

Daniel took the piece of paper and put it in his jacket pocket, before reaching into his bag and pulling out a CD.

'For you ... maybe your wife would listen to it ... she might even like it ... Now I really must go. Good to meet you, Mr Mautner.'

'I hope to see you at the club, Daniel'

'Yes, definitely, see you there. Hope you enjoy the CD.'

—

As Daniel made his way back to the station the skies suddenly opened, washing the dust and dirt of north-west London from the air. Within seconds he had the High Street to himself. He turned up his collar and put his hands in his pockets. As he did so he felt the piece of paper given him by Mr Mautner and absent-mindedly screwed it up. Fifty-five pounds, only two nutters, and he'd beaten the rain. Not a bad day! He'd certainly be coming back, but not tomorrow. Tomorrow, maybe Horsham. Horsham was easy, if he could get there early enough to claim a pitch. Very white English middle-class; his ideal audience. Nothing complicated, no tradition, probably no CD sales either, but he usually made over fifty quid before lunch, and there was a great little diner which served tasty paninis and a large hot chocolate for under a fiver.

—

Josef stayed in the cafe for another coffee as he was in no hurry to get home. His wife had been so angry, so adamant; he hadn't seen her like that in a very long time. And in truth, he didn't really understand it, though he felt that he should. But he had at least done his duty.

He picked up the CD and held it close to his face as he hadn't brought his glasses out with him. *Daniel Trevis, Der Yidisher Fidl.* Beneath the title the young man grinned back at him, mid-bow, wearing a long white peasant-style smock, a flamboyantly embroidered Hungarian waistcoat and Soviet worker's cap. On the back the titles and credits were all written in Yiddish and English, though Josef noted many grammatical errors in the Yiddish. Clearly it was put together by someone with no feeling for the language. But still, at least he had tried; credit where credit's due. And his playing had been truly beautiful, there was no denying that. It had moved him. It had a sincerity to it, a reality, wherever it came from. Perhaps that was why it had disturbed his wife so much: because it spoke directly to the heart, and the Good Lord knows her heart has been closed for many years now. Still, he did what he could to be the loyal husband. Whatever she may feel, however broken she was, he still loved her, or at least the memory of her, of what she used to be. And isn't that the natural way of things, after so many years? Isn't it the same thing really? Even so, for him it was enough, and maybe at his age it was all he could manage.

'I still see that nervous young girl in her eyes.' He said this aloud as he put the CD down and pushed it to the other side of the table, as if returning it to Daniel.

———

Later, as he slowly wandered home, Josef found himself humming the first tune Daniel played. He had recognised it, probably from his childhood, though he couldn't be sure; and Daniel had performed it with great soul. It had that quality of hope mingled with despair that he knew so well, almost as if it had been written especially for him. He hummed it over and over, in time with his footsteps, and soon broke into a quiet mumbled singing that stopped only when he reached the gate to his front garden.

Yes, he thought to himself, he had done his duty, but the young man played very beautifully and he would tell her that.

# Oskar Brantwein Gets a Present

'Rats! Oi! You've never seen so many rats! And every one a feast. If you could catch them that is. And that's not so easy in the dark. And with only one leg?! Ach, the human being is an amazing creature. I lived off those rats for nearly three years. Rats and tins of fruit. Brought by the sewer workers. Polish sewer workers! They were good men. Three years and not a glimpse of daylight! When I finally climbed out I was blind for a week!'

Oskar filled the four empty glasses on the table with vodka and raised a toast.

'L'Chaim, to life, and to rats!'

His three young friends raised their glasses and downed them in one, after which Oskar picked up the bottle and gave it a little shake as if to dramatise its emptiness.

'Of course they never brought us schnapps!' and he chuckled at his own humour.

Tomek took the cue and headed across the dreary lounge area to the bar.

The Polish-Jewish Club hadn't been redecorated for as long as anyone could remember. Everything inside was dark and heavy, and the lights seemed permanently on half power. But it did have a bar, sold good Polish kosher vodka from the freezer, and the sofas were well worn in and fairly comfortable. As Tomek waited at the bar for Chaim, the club manager, to return from the kitchen freezer with the bottle, he looked up at the many paintings that adorned the peeling walls, pictures of old men with long beards and peculiar hats; pictures of Jews like his parents had described, and always with a slight hint of guilt. Growing up in Poland he had never knowingly seen a Jew; they were a mythical people, from stories set before the war, before the Russians, long before he was born.

Finally Chaim returned with the bottle, but just as Tomek was about to take it Chaim grabbed his hand and leant towards him across the bar.

'Tomek, I owe you an apology. You and your friends.'

Tomek looked startled, and a little confused.

'When you first started coming here I didn't like it. None of us did. We had a meeting. I wanted to get you banned ... We have a history, Jews and Poles, a bad history.' He loosened his grip on Tomek's hand. 'But, you know, sometimes it's not so good to learn from history ...'

Tomek wasn't sure what to say. 'In Poland history was written by the Russians. Not so good for learning.'

'And you have done wonders for Oskar,' continued Chaim. 'After his accident, well, he seemed to lose his spirit. For more than five years he came and he sat and barely spoke a word. We were all worried. He became old overnight. But now, well, having a new audience, you have brought the life back to his eyes.'

'Oskar. He is very funny man. He tells good stories, yes?'

'That he does, that he does.' Chaim smiled.

Tomek took the bottle from the bar. 'In Poland we have no Jews, but we have kosher vodka, kosher milk, kosher water ... It means good, special.'

Chaim nodded, smiled and turned his attention to wiping the bar.

It was early in the evening, and the club was still fairly empty. Tomek returned bearing the fresh bottle to see Oskar unstrapping his prosthetic leg.

'You see. How it turns in three directions. And here. The shocking absorber. A miracle! Not like the first one. Gevalt! It was dreadful. Well meant, but dreadful. Carved from a birch branch by Dr Katz just after he cut off my leg. You see? Yes? Five days crawling through the woods with a bullet in it. It was a mess! When the Partisans found me I was half dead. But Dr Katz, he was a great surgeon. A great man. Even out there in the woods he worked miracles! I think once he cut it off they used it as bait to trap a boar. Yes indeed, we Jews, we ate pig in the woods. We were hungry. Everything is kosher when you're hungry. We even got the rabbi to bless it. He was a good man, Rabbi Dovid. He would bless anything.'

Oskar filled up the glasses from the by now frosted vodka bottle.

'To Rabbi Dovid and Dr Katz. May they never be hungry again!'

They all toasted.

102

'And all that time, do you know what I dreamt of? Every night. Noodle kugl. Hot sweet noodle kugl. Like mother made ... And then, after the war, I married Elsa. And her noodle kugl is the best I've ever tasted. To this day, every week after the Shabbos: noodle kugl. A man couldn't be happier!'

Just then Pawel arrived.

'Ah, Pawel. Go get yourself a glass. We're toasting noodle kugl.' Oskar was on a roll. He filled the glasses, waited for Pawel to return, and then they all toasted noodle kugl.

Pawel sat down, put his bag on his lap and unzipped it.

'I have a thing for you, Oskar.'

'For me? A thing?'

'Yes. For you. A ... present. You were talking us last week of your Yiddish songs, how you say, nigunim? And you can't listen them more because your tape player broke. Well ...' He took from his bag something box shaped and placed it on the table.

'What's all this then?'

'It's a tape player. For to play your tapes. A present for you. It's um, how you say, two-hand? But it works. I tried. It's good.'

'Well, I am speechless. Thank you. Thank you! You are a good man, Pawel. May the Lord send you many children! And all of them hard workers! ... Elsa will be so happy.' There was a brief moment's silence before he refilled the glasses.

'Let's all drink to that! To Pawel, to nigunim, and to my Elsa's happiness!'

---

The club closed just after half past ten. Oskar bid his young friends good night with much joviality and slightly stumbled the two hundred yards back to his flat, a bedsit above Klein's Bakery. He hated it, and he expected to die there, alone, probably soon. And so, on the scale of things, keeping the place clean and tidy had never been a priority. Alex, his social worker, had often tried to arrange for a cleaner to come, but Oskar always insisted, 'They can sort it all out when I'm dead! It won't be long now!'

As he opened the upstairs door he was greeted with the familiar smell of mothballs, rotten gefilte fish and stale pee. He slumped down on the sofa that doubled as his bed, and absent-mindedly put the cassette player on the table in front of him.

'Gevalt! Is this a life?' he mumbled to himself. 'But it was kindly meant. Pawel, he is a good man.'

He looked at the machine and sighed.

And then, before he knew it, his eyes had closed and he was snoring.

—

He woke with a start and looked at his watch. It was 3am. He shuffled himself up onto his feet and made his way to the bookcase, a large dark oak case filled with many layers of books, papers, boxes and various odd objects. 'Where?' he demanded out loud. 'Where did I put you?' Suddenly inspired by a vague recollection, he removed a section of the front layer of books from the third shelf up to reveal a stack of envelopes and packages wedged behind, between the shelves. There, among them, was a brown padded envelope. It was one of many, but he immediately knew which. He pulled it from the pile and slowly made his way to his sofa, slumping down like a sack of damp flour, and sat there for a few minutes, still, and in silence, before finally taking a deep breath, mumbling something inaudible; and then opened the still-sealed package. He knew what it was from the logo on the front and the sound it made when he shook it. He had known when it arrived five years ago, as soon as he picked it up from the floor.

'Ach, Alex. You are a fool and a yente!' Then he added more gently, 'But what can you possibly know, you're barely more than a child.'

He sat there for a moment, lost in thought, before pulling a letter from the package.

*'Dear Mr Brantwein*

*Further to the enquiry made on your behalf by Mr Alex Bantry, I am pleased to confirm that Mrs Eva Brantwein, your mother, did indeed record an interview with us on 7th September 1969, specifically regarding her and her husband's escape from Prague during the Nazi occupation, and the following years adapting to English culture. This was part of a major drive to document the stories of refugees from the war who had settled in Britain, which took place between 1967 and 1972. We are pleased to enclose a transfer of this interview onto audio* cassette. *If you have any further enquiries please don't hesitate to contact us.*

*Yours sincerely,*
*David Bennings*
*Head of Research and Archives*
*The Imperial War Museum.*

He took the cassette out of the packet and placed it in the tape machine, then pressed play. There was a quiet clunk and a few moments of hiss, before a thin and muffled voice ...

*'So, Mrs Brantwein, I suppose we should start before the occupation. Could you tell us a little about your life, before the Nazis invaded?'*

*'Well, you see, we didn't have much, but it was a good life. My husband was ...'*

Oskar turned off the tape. He hadn't heard his mother's voice for nearly twenty five years. It shocked him. He had forgotten how thick her accent was, and her quaint Yiddish intonation. But it wasn't just that. It was what she was saying, or was about to say. Neither she, nor his father, had ever told him anything about the times before they had arrived in England, before he was born; nor how they got there. They wouldn't speak of it. And he had learnt at an early age not to ask. Yet here she was, talking openly, and to a stranger. Oskar crossed his arms and stared at the machine for some minutes. 'Too soon we grow old, too late we get smart,' he muttered, remembering his mother's voice as he mouthed the words. Finally he took the tape from the machine and put it back in the package. He'd return it to the shelf in the morning.

——

Later that night he dreamt of noodle kugl for the first time in many years.

# One Day in Jerusalem ...

David looked up at the walls of the Old City. It was like an immense medieval castle, desert yellow against an azure sky, just like in the brochures. And this was the middle of December! He searched the sky for exotic birds, eagles or vultures or such, but was disappointed. Behind him a car honked its horn; he hadn't realised he was standing on a road, it was little more than a track, and so quickly returned to what he assumed must be the footpath. To his left he could see far across the valley, eccentrically piled with small clumps of modern houses all built of the same yellow sandstone; to his right a steep bank rising high above him, overgrown with thorny bushes and topped by the Old City wall. Running between the two, twenty or so yards away, was a main road, three lanes in each direction, completely choked and almost stationary. David took out his camera and tried to frame the juxtaposition of ancient and modern, but the scale was too big for his lens.

The footpath turned to rise diagonally up through the bushes until it joined a wider track-way along the base of the Old City wall. From this higher vantage point the skyline on the other side of the valley was punctuated by golden onion domes, church spires and minarets. Fifty yards on, the track-way was joined by a second path and widened out into a proper tarmacked road. Coming towards him was a young Arab-looking man dressed as Father Christmas, his hat and beard tucked into his belt. He was leading a camel heavily laden with boxes labelled 'Christmas Crackers' in English, Hebrew and Arabic, or so David assumed – he could read only the English. This time he waited for the man to pass before taking out his camera. In the distance a muezzin sang the call to prayer and was soon joined by others from every direction.

Just as he was approaching the Damascus Gate his phone rang. It was Avi.

'Hey David. Good to hear you. And welcome to Israel! Everything is good, I hope?'

'Yeah, just at the Damascus Gate. Taking it all in.'

'Good. Listen David, the traffic out of Tel Aviv was terrible. I won't get to you for another hour or so.'

'No problem. I'm sure I can occupy myself. I'll go for a little wander.'

'Yeah, there's a lot to see. But don't go getting yourself lost. It's a bit of a maze.'

Actually he was quite pleased to have the chance to explore on his own. He'd heard a lot about Jerusalem. Everyone said it was a crazy place.

The Damascus Gate opened out onto a small square. To the right were a number of handcarts piled high with breads, corncobs, pretzels, pomegranates, avocados; and smaller stalls perched on makeshift stands, brewing up cardamom coffee and minted tea. At the far end a crowd of large Nigerian women in loud print dresses were being called to order by their tour guide. Not really sure where he was going, David wandered towards the stalls but, before he was even half way across, a voice caught his ear.

'English! ... English!'

David stopped and turned around to see a short plump Jewish man, about fifty, wearing a skullcap and a navy blue suit, heading towards him.

'You are English?'

'Yes ...'

'So tell me, where in England are you from?'

'London. A place called Golders Green,' he replied, trying to convey the tone of someone who was on his way elsewhere.

'I visited England, twenty years ago it was. You know Manchester?'

'I've been there, once.' David was unsure where all this was going, but was beginning to feel cornered.

'A great city. Very grand. You like football?'

'Not really.'

'I thought all English liked football.'

David shrugged.

'So! My name is Moishe.' He held out his hand and David shook it.

'David.'

Moishe didn't let go. 'David, a good name. And you are Jewish?'

'Yes.'

'On holiday?'

'Well, no, not really. I'm here for a conference.' David wanted his hand back and tried to gently pull it free but Moishe tightened his grip.

'Oh, what is it you do?'

'Interactive databasing.'

'Computers, yes?'

'Yes. Programming databases to network.'

'But today you are on holiday?'

'I guess so.'

'To see Jerusalem, the Old City …' Moishe was still holding his hand. 'Come, David, I have something I would like to show you.'

David again tried to pull his hand free. 'I really just wanted to go for a walk.'

'No come, I'll show you …' and he started to drag David by the hand across the square, but this time David stood his ground.

'What is it you want to show me?' he demanded politely.

'You'll be buying presents, yes? I have a little shop, just over there, a schmutter shop. You take a look. Maybe you'll be my first customer of the day.'

'I'm really just looking around.'

'Sure, come, take a look. If you like, you buy. If not, we stay friends.'

David gave in. It couldn't do any harm, and Christmas was coming up; he did need to get some presents.

Finally confident that he would be followed, Moishe let go of David's hand and led him across the square and down an alley to a small lock-up. He unlocked and raised the metal grill, opened the door and gestured for David to go in first. As David stepped into the dark he did wonder momentarily if it was a good idea to go off with a stranger down an alley and into a lock-up. He'd think twice in London, and this was the Middle East. But as the lights flicked on he was reassured to see glass shelves packed with candlesticks, jewellery displays, little statuettes of dancing violinists, framed paintings of Jewish folk life. It was all too familiar: there were three shops along Golders Green High Street with the exact same stock.

'Please, take your time, look around ...' Moishe was busying himself behind a glass counter.

Ten minutes and a long hard sell later, David emerged, embarrassed and a little irritated at himself. He stuffed the bag with his reluctant purchases – a pashmina and a supposed Bedouin ring – deep into his jacket pocket and headed back up the alley, doing the maths in his head: one hundred and fifty shekels – Jesus, that's twenty-five pounds.

It was with some relief that he found himself back at the square, only now he was wary. He looked at his watch. Avi would be here in about twenty minutes. Perhaps he wouldn't wander any further for now. Perhaps he would buy a cup of pomegranate juice and a roasted corncob, and sit on the steps by the Old City wall. He might see some interesting birds from there.

———

The corncob was delicious: fresher, crispier and sweeter than any he had tasted, but the pomegranate juice left a slightly bitter taste in his mouth. Occasionally he looked up to scour the sky for birds, but saw nothing of note, except for two pigeons, hopping around the rubbish bins, with a slightly different colouring to those back at home. He made a mental note: pinkish breast with orange flecks, and a black bar along the edge of the wing; he'd look it up when he got back. A few yards away an Arab tradesman was setting up a stand selling nuts and dried fruit, and in the middle distance the steady stream of traffic periodically erupted in an impatient chorus of honking. He checked his watch: two-fifteen; Avi should be here any minute. Searching the crowds for his friend's familiar face he noticed a group of crows sat on the city wall – hooded crows, their grey waistcoats ruffled in the gathering breeze. He watched them squabble over a piece of pretzel until his attention was diverted by an unexpected smell: the man at the nut stall was roasting sugared almonds, drenching the air in a sticky sweetness.

'David!' Avi's voice shook him from his reverie. 'David, my old friend, how good to see you. You're looking great. It's been what? Seven years?'

'Something like that. And you too ...' David stood up and Avi gave him an enormous bear hug which he tried awkwardly to reciprocate.

'So, how are you liking Israel?'

'It's great. It's weird actually. One minute it feels just like Golders

Green, then something bizarre appears, like a camel, or soldiers with machine guns.'

'Well, we do like to surprise. They put you up in a nice hotel, yes?'

'It is pretty nice, I have to say.'

'You see, you are a success!'

'I guess so, in a way.'

'You're too modest.'

'I'm English!'

'Yes, but you're also Jewish.'

'Not really,' David insisted.

'David, I've known you since you were six. You're an old Jew and you always will be.'

There was a brief pause which David filled by sitting back down on the step. Avi joined him.

'So, which way shall we head? I've brought a map.'

Avi took the map from David and opened it out.

'Okay, so we are here, at the Damascus Gate … Where did you get to earlier? Did you see the Jewish Quarter?'

'Just hung around here really. I thought it would be more fun to wait for you, you know, before exploring. I was hoping to see some good birds. Do you know if you get any eagles or vultures round here? It looks like good raptor territory, what with all the hills and scrubland.'

Avi laughed. 'I'd forgotten about your bird-spotting. Haven't you grown out of that yet?'

'Is it something I should grow out of?'

'So,' Avi continued, 'if you look at the map the Old City is divided into four main quarters: Jewish, Christian, Armenian and Arab. You see how big the Arab Quarter is? Nearly half! That's how greedy they are. Only ten per cent of the population and yet they claim half the city!'

'What should I see? I mean, what do you suggest? And not just the tourist stuff.'

'Well first, of course, you have to see the Wailing Wall – the only place in the world where Jews go crazy like the rest of them. And the Dome on the Mount is extraordinary. Then I thought we might head to the Christian Quarter for some food. There are some very good Ethiopian restaurants. What do you say? You like Ethiopian food?'

'Sounds good to me.' He didn't know what Ethiopian food was, but remembered someone else telling him it was good.

Avi stood up and clapped his hands to signal the start of their journey. As they crossed the small square David was relieved to see no sign of Moishe.

'It's funny,' he said, 'every year I go to my folks for Passover and we all sit around the table toasting "next year in Jerusalem", but I never thought I'd actually get here, not for any reason, let alone a databasing conference.'

'And you say you're not Jewish!'

———

They entered one of the many narrow market streets that led off the square and were suddenly engulfed in a chaos of competing cultures and iconography, all spilling out of the open-fronted shops, onto the cobbled pavements, and on down the hill. Armenian embroidered robes hung next to Nike T-shirts; Roman antiquities beside cheap electronics; trays of pungent spices and plastic Jesuses amidst rolls of Persian carpets and handmade leather handbags, piles upon piles; and everywhere, tourists, of all hues and shapes and sizes, milling about, handling the goods, haggling with shopkeepers in a hundred different languages, or so it seemed. As they pushed their way through the bustling crowds someone shouted out 'English!?', causing David to look around.

'Ignore them. They all do that, to see who looks up. The English are famously easy for hustling.'

They continued on down the hill where the street met another slightly wider street, filled with the same shops, the same tourists, and the same pushy tradesmen. Three youthful soldiers stood at the junction, chatting among themselves, two boys and a girl, their machine guns slung casually across their backs.

'Is it safe to wander round here?' David asked a little nervously. 'You know, bombs and all that.'

Avi laughed. 'Is it safe anywhere? But seriously, this is probably the safest place in the whole of the Middle East. You see how many soldiers there are? On almost every corner. And they're all specially trained for Jerusalem. You just try doing anything that looks at all suspicious – you'd be surrounded within seconds. And the Arabs know it. There hasn't been a bomb in here for over thirty years. And when you think about it, that's quite an achievement. No?'

David looked back at the soldiers. The girl was so short that the tip of her gun dragged on the cobbles as she moved.

'You have to understand,' Avi continued, 'we are at war here. We're strong because we have to be, and they respect us for it.'

They continued on in silence through the maze of market alleyways, and eventually followed a sign to a tunnel, guarded by a small army checkpoint. Avi exchanged a few words with the soldiers, then called for David to follow him through the barrier.

'We're lucky, the Wall is pretty empty on Sunday afternoons. Normally this place would be heaving with Chassids.'

The tunnel opened out into a large vaulted foyer, flanked on either side by great sandstone arches. Along the walls upmarket shops displayed Hebrew books and scrolls, prayer shawls, tefillin, silver candlesticks, all the accoutrements of Jewish ritual. The shops looked expensive and were all empty.

They crossed the foyer and came out into a great square, made all the larger by its plainness.

'So, there you have it,' said Avi. 'The holiest site for all Jews: the Wailing Wall.' He gestured to the largest of the three walls.

'Well, for a wall it's quite impressive, I guess ... It's big ...'

'Of course it's not about the Wall. It's the Temple Mount itself. The Wall is all the Arabs let us have. And in the interests of peace, we go along with it. But look up there.' He gestured above the Wall, to the left. 'What do the Arabs do? They build a mosque right on the top, just where the Temple is prophesised. Because we have the patience to wait! You see what they are like?'

'That was thirteen hundred years ago.'

'So? How much has changed?'

As he got closer to the Wall he realised that actually it was quite impressive. The lower thirty feet were made of immense sandstone blocks, some as tall as a man and twice as long, carved with deep grooves by many centuries of rain and wind. Here and there surprisingly large bushes had taken root in the cracks. The top twenty feet was made up of smaller blocks, no doubt of a later date, probably medieval. Along the bottom were occasional office-type tables and white plastic garden chairs, and in front of them, all along the base of the wall, was a row of men, only men, some Chassids, some in prayer shawls, some in jeans and T-shirts, but all wearing skullcaps, and all facing the wall, muttering to themselves whilst rocking back and forth. He had intended to approach the Wall, to touch it, just for the sake of it, but now he was here that felt somehow inappropriate, so he stopped about a metre away and watched the nodding Jews go about their rocking. Every now and then one of them would slip a rolled-up piece of paper into a crack, then continue with his rocking and mumbling. David recalled seeing men pray like this at his grandmother's funeral. He had found it bizarre at the time, though in the circumstances it had added to the sombre ritual of the event, but here it felt altogether stranger and poignant; such earnest prayers before not even a ruin so much as a remnant, a fragment. And up above, the glistening of the golden dome, as if to rub it in. He returned to the barrier where Avi was waiting.

'So did you notice our direct postal system to God?'

David looked puzzled.

'The notes in the wall ...'

David smiled at the badness of the joke and they headed back towards the foyer.

'What's the rocking all about?'

'Just Jews being crazy. You haven't seen anything yet, my friend. Jerusalem is a strange place. Attracts all the weirdoes. There's a hospital on the edge of town filled with crazies thinking they're the Messiah. I tell you, there's something about Jerusalem, maybe it's the rock, that gives off a freaky energy or something, who knows? But there's definitely something about Jerusalem. Makes people go mad.'

—

Before long they were back among the maze of alleys, heading into the Arab Quarter in search of a route up to the Dome. Avi strode ahead, occasionally pausing to look at the map, whilst David lagged behind a little, slowing here and there to take it all in. The Arab Quarter was far emptier, more ramshackle, run-down, with fewer shops – little more than market stalls – selling practical goods, cheap T-shirts, second-hand shoes, piles of unwashed root vegetables, and with bags of rubbish dumped in corners. Here people were going about their ordinary

114

business: men pulling handcarts, delivering goods; women buying food, some carrying bundles on their heads; children playing tag, kicking balls. For the first time David felt he was somewhere genuinely foreign, like the Arab villages he saw on the news, usually when bad things had happened. But then again, it wasn't really unlike some areas in London, certainly no poorer or dirtier. Maybe it was the light, and the yellow stone, the feeling of age. The tourist streets had been so crowded that he hadn't noticed the buildings themselves. Not that there was much to notice. Just high walls on either side, worn smooth by centuries of hands and shoulders, occasionally breaking into arches, and here and there, rusted metal doors giving no indication of what might lie beyond. Periodically the narrow alleys turned into tunnels as newer buildings had been stacked on top, piling up over the centuries.

After having to go back on themselves a number of times, Avi declared the map to be inaccurate, and followed his instincts instead, which proved equally haphazard. When they finally found the entrance they were met by an army checkpoint, and this time Avi's questions were not greeted with the required answers and the discussion soon took a louder, more aggressive tone. David had seen this before: Israelis discussing. When it became apparent that they wouldn't be allowed in he knew what to expect.

'You see!' Avi almost shouted as they headed off. 'What did I tell you?! We let the Arabs go wherever they see fit in Jerusalem. Even the Wailing Wall, if that's what they want. And what do they do? They say only Muslims can visit the Mount. Our holiest site, only Muslims. And to them it's only the third holiest. You see what they are like?'

'You don't believe in all that holy shit anyway,' David objected.

'Since when was that the point? What I believe doesn't matter. It's the principle!'

David again tried to change the subject.

'Okay, so … food!' His tone was contrivedly upbeat. 'Where are we going?'

Avi took out the inaccurate map and, after a brief discussion, led the way down a long sloping passage. Ahead of them the flow was blocked by a boy attempting to drag four goats along the narrow lane whilst keeping them away from stalls selling food by means of a long stick. People were shouting in Arabic, trying to push past, protecting their goods, generally expressing their impatience. Avi was having none of it and somehow shoved his way through the crowd, dragging David behind him. Even the goats seemed to move when they saw him coming.

'You see,' said Avi once they were through, 'you've just got to be firm with them. That's all it takes.'

———

The transition between the Arab and Christian Quarters was surprisingly abrupt, though there was no checkpoint or barrier as David had expected. Here the shops had windowed fronts and the crowds were smartly dressed with cameras around their necks. Everywhere David looked, Jesus and Mary stared back at him, from mugs, T-shirts, clocks, towels, even cans of fizzy drink. Many shops were festooned with Christmas lights and some had Santa displays with fake snow sprayed on the windows and carols playing through tinny loudspeakers. Only the high ancient walls remained the same.

'Where are we heading?' David asked as they reached a relatively empty stretch.

'I know a very special little restaurant, does a wonderful injera ... You've never tasted anything quite like it.'

'And whereabouts is it from here?'

'Up towards the Jaffa Gate ... I'll know it when I see it.'

David was getting hungry, and irritable. All this striding up and down hills had left him a little weak in the legs. He wanted to sit down and drink something sweet, but soon they were halted again by another crowd blocking their way. As they got closer it became clear that this was a religious procession of some kind. The air was rich with incense, bells were being rung, and a low mumbling of Latin echoed around the high walls. David could just catch the pointed tops of white hoods at the head of the crowd, presumably monks' cowls, though from the back they looked very similar to the hoods worn by the Ku Klux Klan. Impatient as ever, Avi was pushing and elbowing his way toward the front, and David followed, but when they reached the procession itself he stopped. It was one thing shoving your way past a trip of goats, but monks demanded a modicum of respect. Avi turned back, looking irritated.

'Come on! If we don't get past now we'll be stuck here for hours!'

David didn't know what to say and so shrugged his shoulders, but before Avi had a chance to respond they were both distracted by a second procession that suddenly appeared ahead of them and was moving in their direction. The people in this new procession were dressed all in black, with tall square hats, and carrying large gold crucifixes mounted on long poles. They were singing loudly, and their harmonies had an exotic flavour. Immediately the tension rose, as both crowds began to shout at each other, picking up their pace, moving head on. Only the monks at the front retained their composure. Avi turned to David again.

'Come on! Let's get past. Something's going to kick off here!'

But David just stood there, not knowing what to do. By now the shouting was taking a more aggressive turn and it was clear neither procession was going to back down. They were only ten yards apart, and the path between them was narrow with no exits. Shopkeepers, hearing what was happening, rushed to close the security shutters on their windows. David tried to make his way back through the crush. Suddenly cans were being thrown in both directions, everyone was shouting, jostling, and he could no longer see Avi in the chaos. Then he lost his footing, falling on top of one of the white-robed monks. For a moment their eyes met, and he was shocked at the anger in the face of this man; he looked almost demonic. As soon as the monk had regained his balance he picked up one of the cans and hurled it back in the direction it came from, shouting something in what sounded like Italian. David had had enough of this and so pushed his way towards the back only to find himself facing a group of soldiers with machine guns and loudhailers, shouting at the crowd to disperse. He turned to look for Avi but all he could see was a tight knot of monks in black and white robes, throwing punches and kicks in all directions. Then a sudden burst of gunfire split the air and people were running, a look of genuine fear on their faces, so he ran too, with all his might, following the others down steps, round corners, and on through the maze of alleys. It can't have been much more than five hundred yards, but when he stopped he was exhausted and slumped against the wall, his heart pounding. As he slowly regained his breath he realised had no idea where he was. Nor where Avi was. He took out his phone. No signal, but there was a message from Avi.

'mt @ jffa gt'.

Okay, so where was that then?

He stood up and looked around. He was in a back-alley, probably in the Arab Quarter. There were few people and no stalls. He tried asking directions from a man who was passing purposefully, a bundle of clothes slung over his back in a net bag, but was greeted with puzzlement and the phrase 'no speaking English'. Then there was nobody. And silence. Not even the sound of distant feet on the cobbles.

—

As soon as he realised he was alone something broke in his composure and he had to sit down again. Suddenly he found he was shaking. 'Fucking hell!' he thought, saying the words out loud. Then he felt like he wanted to cry, but managed to stifle it. He was taking fast shallow breaths and his chest felt tight. For a moment he wondered if he was having a heart attack, but after a few minutes it passed. Then he began to feel angry: angry at the way Avi talked down to him all the fucking time; angry at having been dragged into that fight, riot, whatever you'd call it; angry at having been scared stupid, at running away like a coward; angry at Avi for abandoning him; angry at religion – I mean, what the fuck is all that about? Turns people into fucking animals!

This time when he stood up, he had made up his mind: he'd had enough. He was going back to the hotel, though which way that was he had no idea. He tried heading back the way he had come, but couldn't find the steps he had run down, and none of these passages looked familiar. Or rather they all looked the same. And still there were no people. The Old City isn't big, he thought. You should be able to walk from one side to the other in no more than fifteen minutes. He quickened his pace a little, taking random lefts and rights, but still every passage led only to another, and still he was alone. It was as if he had somehow stumbled into a maze; or perhaps the city itself didn't want him to leave, perhaps it hadn't done with him yet. As he framed this thought he realised how ridiculous it sounded, but even so the feeling remained however much he tried to rationalise it away.

After fifteen minutes of wandering back and forth he still hadn't seen a single person, which was becoming a little creepy, and he was now more lost than before. He'd been trying to get back up a level as he remembered going down some steps, but clearly that wasn't working for whatever reason, so he decided to follow the path down and hopefully, at the bottom, he would find another route. Wherever he was, the passages here were narrower, damper, mustier, and the walls on either side were taller, plainer, and seemed very old. Occasional windows here and there were boarded up with rusty metal shutters. As he walked the silence was broken only by his own footsteps, which were uncomfortably loud, so he tried to place them more gently, but still the leather soles seemed to clatter on the cobbles.

The further he went the more ancient seemed the walls and arches, and as he approached the bottom of the hill he passed Roman pillars – some toppled, some still standing, all left where they were and built around – and later the entire front of a temple that had been filled in and used as foundations for whatever rested above. Suddenly David realised how dark it had become. The walls on either side were so high that even now, in the early afternoon, the sun couldn't reach. There was now a thick mustiness in the air, and when he accidentally brushed against a wall it felt cold, and a little damp. It was as if he had entered some kind of netherworld beneath the city itself. Finally the alley levelled off and passed into a long tunnel. At the far end something was flickering in pink light. At first he assumed it must be some kind of Christmas display, but as he got closer the air began to hum with the electric buzz and crackle of fluorescent tubes. It was a sign, the kind of sign that would have been more at home amongst the seedy backstreets of Soho advertising girls – three lines in three languages, in glowing pink neon tubing, imitating handwriting above a rusted metal door. The lower line, in English, read, 'You Are Expected' … As he got closer he noticed that the door was slightly ajar and he couldn't resist taking a peek inside, but just as he was leaning in towards the gap the door swung open, nearly pushing him over.

'Ah, David, we have been expecting you.'

The short round Chassidic man burst into laughter. 'That was a good one, your face, yes, very good.'

David just stood there, his jaw hanging open like an imbecile.

'I'm sorry. My name is Gavriel. And don't worry, David, it's no magic. You have an ID badge inside your jacket. I saw it, so I say 'David'. And this is the You Are Expected door, so I say you are expected. It's my little joke. But your face … very funny, yes?'

David didn't know what to do or say.

'So, David, come in.'

'Ermm, I'm looking for the Jaffa Gate.'

'I know, I know. Please come in. This is a good place. A secret place. But you, you have found it, so you must come in.'

'No, really, I am meeting a friend.'

'Your friend, he will wait. You'll see. But this you should not miss.'

The man had a small head packed with oversized features, lending his smile the appearance of a Cheshire Cat. Hanging in front of his ears were long Chassidic curls yet he wasn't wearing a skullcap, which surprised David. He had never seen a Chassid without his skullcap. But then he seemed friendly, and David was a little curious at what might lie beyond the door.

'Well, okay,' he said, 'just for a minute, though. I really ought to be getting on.'

'Good, good! You'll see. It will be worth it. It will all be worth it, in the end. And in any case, the quickest way to where you are going is right here. Really. You'll see. You'll see.'

As David stepped through the door he was surprised to find himself in a garden, with palms, orange trees and grape vines set around the edges. At the centre was a large Romanesque fountain, and all about people were sitting in small groups, talking, playing board games, smoking hubba-bubba pipes, generally looking relaxed.

'You are surprised, yes? Everybody is surprised the first time. But still I think you have not yet seen. Look around, more closely. This is very special place.'

Suddenly it struck him. It was the people, all kinds of people: Arabs, Jews, Christian monks, Japanese tourists, everyone, sat around together in little groups, as if friends.

'Now I think you are understanding. You see, this is a holy place, the holy place, before Jesus, before David, even Moses – this place has always been blessed. That's why they built the temple here in the first place, why Jesus had to die here. Here it is so holy, so close to God, all gods, not just the Jewish god, that here you do not have to try. It is Jerusalem's best secret, yes?'

David had no idea what this little man was talking about. Where the hell was he? And should he be here at all? Was it safe? That was the question. And where was the exit?

'What do you mean?' he said to cover his brewing anxiety.

'Here you don't have to try. All those rules, strictures, you know – pray five times a day, cover your head, don't eat pork, hate this person, love that person, do this, don't do that – in this place none of that matters, because being here is enough. For God, for man, for everyone – done.'

'Okay, so ... errmm ... I don't know ...'

Gavriel laughed.

'Of course you don't, David. Nobody does. But, look around you ... You see over there.' He gestured with a short stubby hand. 'That's Nissa, with Feival and Kaleb.'

David saw a woman, in headscarf and veil, playing cards with a young Chassid and an Israeli soldier.

'Outside she wears that veil because she has to, not to do so would mean disgrace. But in here she wears it because she wants to. You see? That is the difference. And in here she also gambles, and drinks martinis. And sometimes we all dance together.'

David's instinct told him this was all nonsense, but then the evidence of his eyes said otherwise. It was like a scene from a Coca-Cola advert: all creeds, all nations, living together in perfect harmony. Come on, that's ridiculous. It must be a setup.

'No, David, it's no setup. This is for real. You'll see.'

Now that was creepy. He was sure he hadn't said that out loud. But stranger still, though his mind told him that this was not in keeping with his understanding of reality, and really he ought to be panicking by now, or at least on high alert, he felt entirely at ease. His anxiety had disappeared. It was as if he were observing all the weirdness, whilst actually feeling relaxed within it; and that wasn't like him. Had they drugged him? Was he dreaming? Maybe he had had a knock on the head or something, at the riot: that would make sense, and all of this was his unconscious struggling to find its way back to the surface.

'Listen, David, your head is never going to get this. It just isn't equipped. You see, the ways of God are not for us to understand any more than the ways of man are grasped by the flies that buzz about our food. But they know it tastes good ... Hmm, that may not perhaps be true, but it works ... So, you must listen to your heart. Does it not tell you that everything here tastes good? So why question? We do not know how, or why, but it *is*, and that should be enough, yes?'

By now they had crossed the garden and passed through a Roman portico into an enormous hall, supported by great stone pillars and decked out like a Bedouin-themed restaurant, complete with a camel yawning grumpily in one corner. The walls and ceiling were hung with patterned fabrics and ornamented metal lanterns; the floor, covered with cushions and carpets. At the far end was what looked like a buffet. Here and there small groups of people were sat around in circles, eating, drinking, talking, and one group was singing.

'So, are you hungry?'

David was hungry, but felt he ought to wait.

'The thing is I'm supposed to be meeting my friend for lunch, at the Jaffa Gate. That's what I was looking for when –'

'When you found us, yes? Tell me, David, if your friend, what's his name, Avi is it? So, if Avi had stumbled into this special place, would he be rushing off to meet you? I think perhaps he is not such a good friend as this.'

There was some truth in that, and if he were honest, he was in no hurry to get back to Avi. He had begun to find him a little irritating, much more than he used to. Or had he just forgotten how irritating he can be? And patronising too. And the food did smell delicious. So, much to his surprise, he agreed.

As they made their way to the buffet, weaving a path around pillars and people, David noticed two men, in monks' robes, sat to his left, sharing a hubba-bubba pipe, one robed in black, the other in white. He wondered if they were the same denominations as the monks at the riot.

Gavriel had followed his eyes.

'Yes, that's Gregoris and Abdul. Outside they are very angry. I think it's a dispute about rights to process, or something. I never really listen; it's all very boring. But in here they are good friends. On karaoke nights they sing duets together. Just so long as they don't leave together ...' He let out a short self-congratulatory burst of laughter, as if he had said something very funny.

'You see, David, in here, it is impossible to be angry. You just try it. Go on, think of the thing that makes you most angry. Perhaps your divorce, yes? Think of your ex, Clare, in bed with ... Tom ... that's his name, isn't it? ... Tom with his fat baldy smug grin ... You see? ... You are hoping they are happy together, yes? You have never felt that before now have you?'

He was right again.

'You see. It is all as I said. Here we are in the Good Lord's Grace.'

David was getting used to this odd little man reading his thoughts. Somehow it felt quite normal, natural, not at all strange or magical as it should; as ordinary as, well, talking.

'Now, food. Come, help yourself – it's all good, especially the pork … Such a shame, no other meat crackles quite like pork. I tell you, David, if Judaism had been born in the woods …' He left the sentence in the air as he was suddenly distracted by the appearance of a huge white-bearded man striding purposefully, though daintily, across the hall towards the buffet. He was at least eight feet tall and seemed to be dressed up as God – white-robed, a staff in one hand, a set of scales in the other. Gavriel immediately approached him, addressing him loudly in a slightly patronising tone.

'Eric, please, haven't we talked about this already?'

He turned back to David.

'I'm sorry, I have to speak with him. I'll be right back … Eric, what did I say to you? You have to be careful in here. People don't know quite what to expect. And wandering around dressed up like that? Sometimes they get confused. You should hear the stories. Come on, at least put down the scales. In any case how are you going to hold your plate? Yes? Now come with me, we'll put them in the safe, and you can collect them on the way out. Yes? Come along …'

David couldn't hear the giant's mumbled response above the general hubbub, but it was clear he had submitted, for the two of them headed off together towards a side passage.

Just as he was about to wonder what he should do now, the smell of food reminded him. He turned back to the tray of what looked like barbecued ribs. It all smelt so good. After due consideration of the many options, he took a plate from the side and piled it with pork fritters, garlic-fried pigeon breasts in what smelt like an apricot sauce, spiced lemon couscous, mixed roasted vegetables, and sour cucumber salad, salted and sugared exactly like his grandmother used to make. Once his plate was full he turned around but, before he could wonder where to sit, his attention was attracted by a small group of people, sat about five metres away, who were beckoning him towards them. Instinctively he looked behind him, over his shoulder, then back at the beckoners. Yes, they did seem to mean him. There were four of them: a woman in her mid-twenties, quite attractive, with short brunette hair, wearing a nun's habit, her pleated wimple neatly folded on a cushion beside her; a younger man, probably aged around twenty, in an Israeli soldier's uniform, his gun laid across his lap – he was stroking it like a cat; an older skinny, bare-chested man with a long grey beard, straggly shoulder-length hair, and an unpredictable look in his eyes – he reminded David of a comedy hermit from a Monty Python film; and an American tourist, complete with loud checked blazer and what was presumably a ten-gallon hat – it was pretty large in any case. Around his neck was an equally oversized camera. It struck David that they were all such stereotypes, but then he considered his own clothes: Levi's jeans, an Alienware T-shirt and Armani jacket – every bit the IT professional cliché in his own way.

As he headed towards them he was surprised not to find their welcoming smiles at all creepy. In any other situation he would have run a mile from such a scene. But here he somehow felt part of it, as if he were meeting old friends. Very odd.

'Come, sit down, join us,' said the nun.

'Yes, we could do with some new input,' said the soldier, with a slightly pointed tone.

'Ignore him, he's just being funny,' said the nun.

David sat down, placing his food on the low table at the centre of their little group.

'I'm Anita, this is Monesh ...'

'Hi,' said the soldier.

'Ishmael ...'

The bare-chested, bearded man grunted an acknowledgment. Now he was closer, David noticed that he was wearing a loincloth.

'... and Ronnie'.

'Well howdy-do,' said the American in a broad Texan accent.

'I'm David ... from England.' He didn't know why he added that last bit.

'Hello, David from England,' said the nun. 'I see you've met Gavriel.'

'Gavriel? Oh, yes.'

'I hope he didn't freak you out – he does love doing the introductions, the theatricality of it all.'

'So, can you all do that, the mind-reading thing?'

'No,' laughed the nun. 'No, that's just Gavriel. He used to be a mesmerist, in Russia. We're all sure it's just trickery, though no one's worked out quite how he does it yet.'

'Oh, well he had me fooled.'

'Yes, he's very good', said the soldier.

'And all the other stuff, the God stuff?'

'Well that's the big question, isn't it?' She turned her palms up and her gaze heavenward in an exaggeration of questioning. 'What is it with this place?' she declared melodramatically. 'What the fuck is it with this place!?'

At that, the rational part of David, the part that had taken a back seat and was detachedly observing events from a distance, suddenly choked: a nun has just shouted fuck! But the other part of him, the part that was engaged with the conversation, barely noticed.

'She does that just because she can,' explained the soldier. 'She's just showing off.' This was clearly aimed at the nun, who responded by blowing the soldier a kiss.

'Honestly, we don't know. Nobody knows. I don't suppose anybody ever has known.'

'So is that a known unknown, or an unknown unknown?' said the Texan. 'Or perhaps even an unknown known?' He guffawed and slapped his thigh in amusement at his own joke. 'You see, in here I can be funny. Always wanted to be funny. Out there, dry as an ox bone in the desert.'

'So, tell us, David,' said the nun leaning forward towards him, 'what's your tragedy?'

'What? What do you mean?'

'Well, Monesh was just saying that one of the things that draws us all here is our tragedy. But Ishmael pointed out that all of our tragedies are born here, that had we never known of here, we would not be so tragic. So I was wondering, what's your tragedy? Maybe it will help shed some light on these things.'

'I'm not sure I have a tragedy. I … what do you mean by tragedy?'

'Okay, so let's have a group therapy moment. Sit up everyone.' She clapped her hands to get everyone's attention. 'Good. So, my name is Anita, and my tragedy is that in here I am in love with Monesh, but out there we're enemies, and I don't mean in a Romeo and Juliet way, we really do hate each other. And anyway, I'm a nun, for fuck's sake! But somewhere, underneath it all, we know, and that is our tragedy. Don't we, Monesh?' Monesh nodded dutifully. 'Okay, your turn.'

'Ermm, my name's Monesh, and Anita's just said it all … as ever! Plus, out there I take too many drugs and get off on shooting at Arabs.'

'Well, you're young,' said the man in the loincloth. 'Which young man doesn't enjoy the opportunity to shoot off his gun, eh?'

The Texan laughed.

'Your turn, Ronnie.'

'Hell, okay. My name's Ronald D. McCleash the Third, and I guess my tragedy is that out there I'm real gullible. I mean real gullible. I believe everything I'm told, so long as I'm told it in a good ol' American accent. And you know that wouldn't be so bad, but in here I *know* it's all a pile of hog shit. And that bleeds through a little, so I'm beginning to have myself some doubts. And if there's one thing I was brought up to guard against, them's doubts. Gives me a right ol' pain in the head, I can tell ya.'

'Ishmael, come on, your turn.' She said this in a tone of voice that left him no other recourse.

'Alright, if your holiness insists … My name is Ishmael.' He spoke in a non-participatory monotone. 'My tragedy is that out there I believe the end of the world is imminent. And so I deprive myself of all of the world's comforts and live off alms, dressed in a loincloth, and its bloody cold out there at this time of year! Then, when I come in here I see the complete and utter futility of my whole existence, but at least it's warm, and the food is good. Not to mention the company!' Having done his bit he lay down among the cushions in a token gesture of defiance.

'So, David, it's your turn.'

'Um, okay, well, my name's David, and I'm from England … and, um … and I really don't think I have a tragedy.'

'Come on now, David, everybody has a tragedy.'

'No, I really don't think I do … I have a few minor irritations. Maybe some unanswered questions. But honestly, no tragedy.'

'You're sure? You're really sure?'

'Yes. I believe I so.'

'Any unfulfilled dreams, perhaps? Or heroic failures?' She sounded almost concerned.

'None that I can think of. I did once want to be a rock star, but I had no talent for it. Found it all rather silly, to be honest. And it was just a fad, only lasted a few weeks. No, I always wanted to programme computers, since I was a boy, and that's what I do. I guess I am pretty content really.'

The man in the loincloth had sat up again. 'Maybe his tragedy is that he has no tragedy.'

'Yes,' the soldier added. 'That would make sense. To have no tragedy would be a great tragedy indeed. I mean, how would you measure anything? You'd never know what you were dealing with.'

Just at that moment Gavriel appeared behind David.

'David, I do apologise. I just had to speak with Eric, you understand. So, I see you've been getting up to mischief already, yes?' He laughed. 'No, it is my fault. I shouldn't have left you unattended so soon. Come, we must continue our talk.'

David turned to pick up his plate of food.

'No need for that. You have already eaten.'

He did have a hint of aftertaste left in his mouth, and his belly felt satisfied, but he couldn't remember having eaten anything. He hadn't had time.

'Come.' Gavriel offered David a hand to help him up, which he accepted, and the two of them carefully made their way around the various little groups of people, pillars, cushions, plates and trays, back towards the garden, which was now empty.

'You see,' said Gavriel as they sat at a mosaic table underneath a lemon tree. 'You see, how do I explain …? Yes, many people come to Jerusalem … No, that's not it. Okay. Why do you think people come to Jerusalem, David?'

'I don't know. I'm here on a business trip.'

'Yes, but why do most people come here – to Jerusalem, I mean? … For God, yes? And these are people who have faith, yes? But what is faith? Where does it come from? What is it all about? A dream of a better world, a just world, a fair world, of belonging to a world that makes sense, that it is all God's will … You see, all of this, this is dissatisfaction with how things are, and dissatisfaction breeds anger, fear, frustration, and so they find faith, and the greater their anger or fear, the greater their faith, and that's why they come to Jerusalem. Because their faith is everything to them. You understand?'

David nodded, as prompted.

'But in here, in this magic place, there is no anger, or fear, or frustration, or dissatisfaction. It simply cannot be, as you have seen. And so for many people, for most people, entering in here, it is a problem, a tragedy, for them.'

David must have been looking puzzled, as Gavriel proceeded to spell it out more simply.

'Right. Okay. So, it is faith that brings them to Jerusalem, yes? And their faith is born of anger and fear, yes? But it is their life, yes? Their heart. You understand? So they find the door, and they come in here, where there is no anger or fear, etc etc. So what is left?'

David shrugged.

'Now I think you are understanding. So, they check their life, their values, their beliefs, their faith, at the door, when they enter. And whilst in here they see the futility of it all, how they are wasting their lives in misdirection, but all the while they know that they must take it all back as they leave. And then their visit will be like a dream – they will remember the thinking, but their hearts will be closed again. You understand? And that is their tragedy. You see? Their tragedy leads them to faith, and their faith leads them to tragedy ... it is all circles, everything goes in circles. You understand?'

'I think so. But then, why am I here? I have no tragedy.'

'Well that is the thing David. You saying you have no tragedy, it is a little confusing to them. Now I'm not being funny, but you and I both know that people whose passion, whose life becomes their faith, well, they can become a little simple. Don't mistake me, I don't mean stupid, often far from it, but simple, yes. They see the world in simple terms, black and white: Good/Evil; Heaven/Hell; Life/Death; one of us/ not one of us. You know what I'm saying. But you and I, we know that sometimes things can be more complicated than that, yes?'

'Yes. Absolutely.'

'So you saying you have no tragedy, that doesn't fit with them, makes them ask questions, questions with no answers, and, for simple people, questions with no answers require faith, or their world begins to unravel, and not only at the edges, but from the centre out. And *here* there is no Faith, because here *is*. You are following?'

'I think so.'

'So all I am saying is – please, just be a little careful what you say. Think of them as children. It's not their fault. And I have no say over who finds the door. If I did, the Good Lord knows, things would be a little easier around here. But no, I can only oil the wheels, you understand?'

David had given up trying to understand any of this, but found himself nodding nonetheless, as somehow it did make a kind of sense.

'And in any case, David, you do have a tragedy. You just don't know it yet.'

Gavriel stood up.

'Now,' he continued in a more upbeat tone, 'I am thinking that maybe it is time for you to find your friend. Of course you are welcome here always, and I am sure you will be coming back. But for now, I think you have a lot to take in, to think about, and staying here too long can be bad for the . . . how would you say, sanity, yes? Especially the first time.'

Whilst he was talking he began to politely usher David back towards the metal door at the far end of the garden.

'And David, you too will stop believing, when you leave. It will be like a half-remembered dream. But there will be a sign, to help you on your way.'

'What do you mean? What kind of sign?'

'You'll know it when you see it … I've never heard of anyone missing their sign, but then how would they know? If they missed it, I mean. You see? As I said, things always go that way, round in circles. In any case I don't know, I am just the messenger. They told me to tell you there would be a sign, so I tell you … Personally I hope they send you an angel. That's always a good one, very impressive, and not so uncommon as you might think …'

When they reached the door, which was firmly locked with two iron bars across it, David realised he had no idea where he was.

'So how do I get to the Jaffa Gate from here?'

Gavriel shrugged. 'That all depends on where you were when you came in.'

He pulled the bars from across the door, then held out his hand to David.

'As is said, every blessing is also a curse, every curse a blessing. It's all circles within circles.'

Then he leant on the large wrought iron handle of the door with much of his weight until there was a loud clunk, the handle suddenly shifted, nearly knocking him from his feet in the process, and the door swung open to reveal a stone staircase.

'Just follow the stairs to the top and you'll soon find your way.'

———

At first he found the going easy, spurred by relief at having left whatever that place was, but soon he began to tire, and yet the steps went on and on. After a few minutes climbing, occasional small windows let in a little sunlight, though they were too dirty to see through. Soon his pace began to slow, and before long he was stopping every twenty steps or so to catch his breath. Then suddenly, without warning, he was at the top, on a busy Arab market street. Overcome with exhaustion and relief at being back in the world he collapsed against a wall, and sat there, panting and smiling, for some minutes. What the hell was that place? he thought. And those freaks? Jesus! It reminded him a little of when he went for a free lunch at the Hare Krishna temple, only there the food was god-awful. And that crazy little man! Still, Avi had warned him about the crazies. Suddenly he began to laugh out loud. It was all so ridiculous. Really, he should have known better. Still, it was all part of the Jerusalem experience. What was it Avi said? – if you haven't seen the crazies, you haven't seen Jerusalem. Something like that.

Once he had got his breath back he took out his phone – still no signal. So where was the Jaffa Gate? Looking around for someone to ask he noticed a sign, high up on the wall in front of him:

JAFFA GATE
CHURCH OF THE HOLY SEPULCHRE

That was almost too easy, he thought, but just as he was about to head to the right, he hesitated, then looked back at the sign. Maybe a moment of quiet reflection in a church was just what he needed. He may have issues with religion but he had always liked churches themselves. Back home he would often take ten minutes of his lunch break to sit in St Mary Magdalene and daydream about numbers. It was the geometry he enjoyed, the symmetry. Where he sat, at the back by the centre aisle, it was almost perfectly balanced, and he found that calming; more than that, it freed him from distractions, helped him to think more clearly. It was there that he had finally cracked the problem with the ATF encoding matrix, which had won him a promotion, and got him invited to this conference. It was something he could never explain to anyone in words, but for him churches are all about numbers, about the patterns they reveal, the way they interact. At least proper churches, old churches, built by architects who understood. And so he headed to the left.

———

It was easy enough to find, but he was immediately disappointed. Certainly he should have expected the chaos of Jerusalem to be spilling over into the church, but he had at least imagined something grand, impressive, inspiring; something akin to the great cathedrals of England. This building looked more municipal than sacred. The 'crusader façade', as the leaflet he had picked up at the gate put it, was an unadorned wall, with two plain arches, one filled in, and higher up, two small arch-shaped windows. It was more like a Victorian factory building than the 'holiest place in Christendom', and, like everything in Jerusalem, it was encroached upon on all sides, leaving only a small walled square at the front, where groups of pilgrims gathered, many of them, it seemed, weeping.

The interior was architecturally as disappointing as the exterior: a large, plain, windowless dome, letting in the smallest amount of sunlight through a hole at the top. Along the walls were occasional stoic little altars, and low arches leading to narrow passages and stone stairways. Here and there enormous candles stood on giant candelabras, lighting the space with a dim orange glow. Despite the many milling tourists and pilgrims, the hall was so large and unadorned that it felt surprisingly empty and quiet, as if all the sound were being sucked up into the vast space above their heads; not at all the echoey boom he would have expected.

At the centre of the main hall, beneath the dome, was what looked like a giant box, the size of a small room, supported by large iron girders along its outside walls. On one side was a low door, and around it, candelabras, metal barriers, and a number of armed security staff. To the right a long queue snaked its way back around the box and out across the hall. David decided to join the queue; it was clearly the main event.

As he slowly shuffled forwards he realised he must have left the leaflet on the steps outside, so he turned to a young couple behind him, who were quietly talking in French.

'Excuse me,' he asked, 'do you speak English?'

'A little,' replied the man, slightly affronted at having his private conversation interrupted.

'What is it we're queuing for here?'

The young man looked surprised. 'This is the tomb of Jesus, where he resurrected, the first Christian church.'

That would do, thought David. That's got to be worth seeing.

It was another ten minutes before he approached the head of the queue where a short, officious woman in a navy blue security uniform was busy enjoying her authority; searching bags and ordering people to move here, there and faster. Periodically a skinny Greek Orthodox priest, wearing a long black beard and tall pointed hat, appeared through the door of the box, exchanged a few words with the woman, then disappeared back inside. It seemed to be a case of three out, three in, once every few minutes. Some of those coming out were carrying lighted candles. Eventually he reached the front where he too was patted, prodded and scanned before being ushered through the barrier and into the box.

He had had no idea what to expect and wasn't sure if he was surprised to find himself in a small room completely lined with grey and red marble, shaped to imitate pillars, scrolls and occasional angels. At the centre was a low plinth, and upon it, behind glass, a flat piece of rock, with no further explanation. He, and the French couple behind him, were told by the priest, through hand gestures, to stand to the right. At the other end was a low doorway, and this was what they were queuing for. After a couple of minutes, the priest approached the doorway and urged the people within to hurry up. Moments later two middle-aged men appeared, followed soon after by an older woman wearing a headscarf and holding a bunch of lit tapers. Immediately the priest accosted her, shouting and gesticulating; clearly he objected to the large flame she was carrying, and she was, it seemed, equally determined to ignore him, and leave with her prize intact. She tried to push her way past him, but he responded by blocking her exit from the room, standing between her and the door, his arms raised, ranting emphatically, as she began to shout back at him in what David recognised as Russian. Then, suddenly the priest leant forward and, with a surprisingly large and powerful breath, extinguished the flames. There was a brief moment of silence before the woman erupted in a torrent of Russian abuse, at which he moved to the side, grabbed her by the shoulders from behind, and aggressively manhandled her out through the door. David found that rather shocking, in such a place as this, but before he could take it in the priest reappeared and gestured him and the French couple through the entrance, into the tomb.

It was a low room, about the size of a single bed. On three sides it was lined with the same medieval marble; the fourth, the ceiling and the floor were bare sandstone rock, crudely hewn, and much more what David would have expected of a rock-cut tomb. If he remembered his school religious studies correctly, Jesus' body had been placed in a tomb cut into the side of a hill, or was it a quarry? And this, it seemed, was now all that was left of it; a small chunk of rock, built into a box, inside a church, inside the Old City.

To the right was a stone bench, the length of the room, again crudely cut, which must have been where the body itself was laid. The ceiling was too low to stand under, and so David followed the lead of the French couple and knelt, facing the stone bench. Directly in front of him was a candle, which, if his mental picture was correct, would be where Jesus' head might have rested. The French couple were now earnestly praying, mumbling to themselves, their eyes closed, hands clasped, elbows resting on the bench. David wasn't sure what he should do. He had never prayed, in earnest or otherwise. But he didn't want to be disrespectful, to sit and gawk, so he followed suit, clasping his own hands together and closing his eyes; and as soon as his eyes were closed exhaustion hit him, and for just a brief moment his mind began to drift. It was a moment of half-sleep, without time, without space, or even consciousness, save for the sense that he was not alone. Something was there with him, something more beautiful and monstrous and comforting than his mind could grasp, and then it was gone, leaving behind it only the echo of great wings flapping over his head – or was it the robes of the priest who was standing over his shoulder, waving his arms at David to move along? He quickly brushed the daydream from his thoughts. It was hardly surprising. He'd been wandering around for hours, he'd barely eaten, and everywhere there was so much craziness, his head had been filled with so much nonsense.

But even so, he wasn't ready to leave the church yet, so decided to explore some of the many passages and stairways that led off the main hall.

The building proved surprising. Like the Old City itself, it had clearly grown up layer upon layer, with each new claimant over its long history adding their own pieces; a small chapel here, an altar there, some richly adorned with gold and jewels, others plain and Spartan. Every passageway led to another interpretation of Christian worship. He walked up a narrow flight of stone steps to find himself surrounded by medieval paintings of monks processing; along a sloping passageway to enter a treasure trove of bejewelled chalices and candlesticks, lighting a wall of unnaturally proportioned images of the child Christ, each beautifully painted but disturbingly unreal; down an ornately arched corridor into the familiar smell of Catholic incense; through a long, unlit tunnel to find himself startled by a huge sculpture of Jesus on the cross, double the size of life, his tortured grimace more pained than any David had seen. And everywhere the sounds of worship: priests intoning, the low mumble of prayer, bells ringing, monks chanting, congregations singing and responding, and, of course, cameras clicking. It was a kaleidoscope of world Christianity but, even so, in a strange way, it all felt more familiar to David than the nodding Jews at the Wailing Wall. He understood the images, he knew the stories they portrayed, and after the chaos of the city beyond, he did find it quietly comforting.

—

By the time he left, darkness had fallen, lending the street-lit sandstone walls a deep amber against the blue-black of the evening sky. Everywhere was quieter, emptier. The shops and stalls were all now tightly locked up behind steel shutters, and the few people still around were on their way somewhere else. David soon returned to the sign and was about to follow it towards the Jaffa Gate when his phone began vibrating in his pocket. He had a signal again, and an answerphone message from Avi.

'Hi David. I hope you're alright. I'm sure you are. Shame we lost each other. I've tried calling a few times. No signal I imagine. Anyway, it's now half past four, I've been waiting an hour and I just got a call, something's come up at work, so I'm sorry but I have to head off, which is a shame, but you know how it is. So, yes, apologies and everything. I'll call you tomorrow and maybe can meet again during the week. You're free evenings, aren't you? And if you still want something good to eat, I recommend the Shegar. Just ask anyone at the Jaffa Gate. It's a two-minute walk. And make sure you order the injera. It's very good. So, good luck, my friend. Speak soon.'

David was relieved at that. Avi felt like hours ago. It was as if he was somewhere else altogether now, a whole different town; the streets, the passageways and arches, the steps and little squares, Jerusalem itself, all felt different. And it was somewhere he didn't want to share with Avi, or with anyone. Despite his tiredness he just wanted to walk and think; no, not think, experience, take it all in. So he randomly took lefts and rights, vaguely heading up the hill.

Suddenly he took a turn and thought he recognised where he was; perhaps he had walked down here earlier with Avi, when it was bustling with tourists and tradesmen. If so, it was very different now. It had a contemplative feel, almost as if he were still in the church. For the first time he noticed the ground he was walking on. It was cobbled with brick-shaped blocks of grey stone, polished smooth by many centuries of feet. Occasionally it broke into short groups of steps, partitioned by two narrow stone ramps towards the edges, presumably for wheeling handcarts – it was too narrow for anything else. It definitely had the look of Roman engineering, much like the diagrams he remembered from school. Underneath this top layer would be gravel, then larger stones, and the foundations would be a good three feet deep. He could feel its history: how many people must have walked these very stones? Romans, probably Pontius Pilate himself, and Jesus, the disciples, all the first Christians, the crusaders, King Richard and Saladin, the Knights Templar, and of course various Persian conquerors over the centuries, medieval pilgrims, through to David Ben-Gurion and the founders of modern Israel; all of them adding their own tiny lustre to the polish beneath his feet. There really is nowhere in the world quite like this place, he mused. So much passion, desire, anger, conviction, compulsion, delusion and general craziness; and for so long a time. He could almost feel it resonating from the stone all around him. Yes, there was definitely something. He tried to let it wash over him, to allow his rational cynicism to melt away, but was suddenly distracted by the unexpected sound of a revving engine. A veiled Muslim woman was coming up the slope behind him on a moped, its first gear whining aggressively as it struggled on the ramps.

Towards the top of the hill one of the shops was still lit, the owner busying himself with putting away the numerous displays spilling out across the pavement. As David passed, the wiry old man called out to him:

'Come, come in, let me lighten your wallet for you. Be my final sale of the day.' It was said in a chirpy, jokey manner, and he clearly didn't expect a response.

David turned around. He was quite taken by the man's jovial cheek, and thought a memento of the day might well be in order.

'Okay,' he challenged the man, 'what've you got?'

The shopkeeper looked momentarily surprised but quickly switched into salesman mode.

'Yes, come in. See for yourself. I have much beautiful things.'

It was a Christian souvenir shop, filled with every imaginable form of cheap Christian tourist tat. David took his time looking around, casting an eye over crosses and crucifixes of all sizes and materials, some gaudily ornamented in gold-coloured plastic and imitation jewels, others plain, their claim to be made of olive wood from the Mount of Olives stamped along the side. He considered the cheaply rendered reproductions of Russian ikons and numerous plastic models of Jesus and Mary, some with flashing lights, others that glowed in the dark. He shook snow-globes featuring Jesus on the cross, and the Last Supper, watching the snow slowly fall upon impossible scenes, and in one corner found a china nativity set in which all the characters were dressed-up little kittens, which he nearly chose. All the while he was expecting the owner to jump in, putting on the hard sell, but the old man continued quietly packing away the pavement displays, occasionally looking up to check David was still there, smiling broadly and nodding if their eyes met.

Finally he made his choice: a lenticular print of Jesus on the cross – what, as a child, he would have called a hologram, in the days before real holograms became common. The image was taken from a staged photograph, lending a peculiarly disturbing quality to the faux 3D, and when the viewer moved from side to side Jesus opened and closed his eyes; at just the right angle David could make him wink. Somehow it seemed to fit with his experience of Jerusalem; a good metaphor.

Sure enough, the old man had been keeping an eye on him.

'A good choice, very modern. You are Christian?'

'Er, no. No, I'm English.'

'Ah, I like the English. Good manners, very polite. Make for good customers.'

David knew what he meant. 'So, how much is this picture?'

'For you, my final customer of the day, fifty shekels.'

David was about to get out his wallet when he noticed a pile of tea towels by the counter, printed with the image of Jesus' head from the Turin Shroud. He picked one up to look.'

'You like?' The old man sounded surprised.

'Sure, why not'. There was something about its inappropriateness that did indeed tickle him.

'Okay then, for you, I say eighty shekels, for the two, yes?'

The old man took the towel from David, folded it and placed it in a black carrier bag along with the picture, whilst David pulled a one hundred-shekel note from his wallet.

'Keep the change,' he said as he passed the note to the old man, who looked puzzled, as if this was extraordinary.

'What is it with you English? You do not understand business, not at all.' And then he laughed, causing David to smile, and then laugh himself. And in that laughter was a feeling of friendship, of warmth, for neither was laughing at the other, but at the game they were both playing, the little dance they had just conducted together, and its unexpected outcome.

As he continued on up the hill David felt a strange sense of empowerment, of victory. He had conducted business on his own terms and won. Plus he had made an old man smile and laugh at the end of a long day, and that had to be a good thing.

When he reached the top of the hill the passage opened out onto a small square that he immediately recognised. It was where he had been hustled by Moishe earlier. He felt in his pocket for the pashmina and bracelet. There it was. He had forgotten that, it seemed so long ago now, but the memory of it made him smile almost nostalgically.

Finally he crossed the square and headed towards the Damascus Gate. It had been quite a day; a fine little adventure, and no doubt one that he would chew upon for a while yet. Tomorrow would be back to normal, talking databases with his American colleagues, which at this moment felt less exciting than it had earlier. As he reached the Damascus Gate, he hesitated, reluctant to cross the boundary between the Old City and the modern world beyond. He turned briefly to look back, as if to imprint the moment, as if he knew it would somehow be important, then continued on his way, leaving the Old City behind him.

The first thing he noticed after passing through the Gate was the sky. All day he had been surrounded by high walls, catching only brief glimpses of sky here and there between the buildings, but now, beyond the walls, and at the top of a hill, the vast blue-black canopy stretched out before him in all directions, and it was unlike any sky he had seen before. Maybe it was the weather conditions, or that he was surrounded by miles of unlit desert scrubland on all sides, but the stars – there were so many, and so bright, it was intoxicating. These weren't the single points of light he was familiar with, they were scattered liberally all over, like salt spilt across a black tablecloth, forming shapes and patterns, making pictures in his mind. He could understand how the ancients must have felt looking upwards, with no distractions, no real comprehension of what it was they saw: it must have seemed truly miraculous; no wonder they connected the movement of the heavens with such wonderful myths and mysteries. To his left he could see the Milky Way, a vast cloud of luminous dust sprinkled with diamonds, and there, in the middle, right in front of him, the crescent moon, turned upon its back like a boat adrift on a mysterious Arabian sea. He had never seen the moon at such an angle before; it made him realise how far he was from home, which was both exciting and a little poignant. But then, just below it, something caught his eye – a tiny silhouette, barely visible against the night. It was moving in gentle circles directly beneath the moon as if attached by some invisible thread, slowly spiralling down, unravelling as it went. David watched, transfixed, as each circle brought it closer to the earth, and after a minute or so he caught the outline of what looked like a large bird, though he couldn't see enough detail to know of what kind. Still it drifted downwards, and now seemed to be circling directly overhead, its great wings flashing white as they caught the moonlight. And suddenly David was struck: could this be the sign that Gavriel had mentioned? Could it be an angel sent to help him on his way? Or had he just spent too long in Jerusalem? No, of course, it was just a bird, coming in to roost having ridden the thermals all day. But what a bird! The closer it got the more its size became apparent. Finally, with an effortless flap of its enormous wings, it landed upon a post, not ten feet away. It was an eagle, an immense pure white eagle, and it was staring straight back at him.

David had no idea how long the two of them remained still, silent, eyes locked together; it seemed both an eternity and an instant, but more than that, it was as if something passed between them, something inexplicable, something that reached deep inside him, touching his soul.

Then, before he could drink his fill, the spell was broken; the wondrous bird opened out its wings, and with a great flap, took to the air and was gone, leaving only the slightest breath of wind behind it.

# Postscript

*As a child my world was made of questions*
*Of hows and whys and wheres and whos and whens*
*And one man, one giant man held all the answers*
*My father, leather capped, and pipe in hand*

*His footsteps crossed whole histories and nations*
*And all the secrets of the universe*
*And though I couldn't understand the half of what he said*
*He taught me where to look and how it works*

*Then when I 'came a man my world expanded*
*His giant's footsteps almost within reach*
*And we would stride together holding forth about the world*
*Arguing as rabbis in full preach*

*When last I saw my father he had shrunk*
*From bed to chair to bed and back again*
*And though his mind still held all the magic of the world*
*He was far too weak to speak or hold a pen*

*Whoever it was said 'do not go gently ...'*
*Wasn't there that day, or they would know*
*That at the end there's no life left for fighting*
*But only pain, decline and time to go*

*And so he died with dignity and grace*
*Leaving only absence, love and loss*
*And now sometimes perhaps I might wear his leather cap*
*But never could I seek to fill his shoes*